Dominated

By the Boss

by

J.D. GRAYSON

25,000 words

2015 Gray Publishing Paperback Edition

ISBN 978-1511422413

CONTENTS

Visit J.D. Grayson's website to signup for a new release alerts.

Website: www.JDGraysonBooks.com

Twitter: @JDGraysonBooks

Part One

CHAPTER ONE

Ashley Taylor flashed a warm smile, flipping her hair and waving a hand. "Enjoy your four-day weekend, Mr. Cole." The curvy blond crossed her smooth legs, granting the boss a teasing glimpse of sheer underwear. Her 26 year-old thighs sluggishly closed the gap, glistening in pale light.

"You too," Mr. Ethan Cole said, hypnotized by the gesture. The 44-year old man paused, mentally treading the path to vaginal bliss. His lustful gaze was nothing new to Ashley, a constant since her hiring. Frankly, there were more qualified accountants, though none matched her bodily assets.

The day he interviewed her, his thoughts started with blowjobs, graduating to sex, degrading into a type of forced servitude. He remembered their job-training sessions, seduced by her sweet lavender perfume. Whenever he leaned over Ashley, her mouthwatering mounds spanned his attention. However, it was the silhouetted tattoo that truly aroused his imagination.

She would purposely bend over, exposing her permanent secret. Immortalized above her butt-crack, a tattooed tramp-stamp turned his thoughts darker. His innocent employee may not have been so innocent, after all.

In reality, the 6-foot, salt and pepper haired man knew better. *You're her boss,* he silently chastised himself. *Even though our company sells sex toys...I've always forbid sexual fraternization, demanding business before pleasure. Besides, I have no power over a piece of ass like that.* Reaching the exit door, he examined one last thought. *Though if my suspicion pans-out, that power will soon change hands.*

A hopeful grunt sounded from Ethan's throat, as he left the office. Ashley barely noticed, awaiting his exit as well. It was Friday night, and her check was in-hand. Unfortunately for her, it was already spent.

Opening her desk drawer, she brushed the petty-cash box aside. *Been there, done that,* she thought. With her husband out of work, siphoning handfuls of money only bought so many groceries. She originally assured herself, *It'll just be a short time, small amount. Hubby will find work and I'll pay it back.*

Of course, she didn't expect a stagnant economy to collapse into depression. By the end of year one, a different kind of depression overtook her. As her husband's unemployment benefits ended, she was forced to alter fate.

At the six-month mark, petty theft turned into heavy embezzlement. She started with ten thousand, slowly working her way up to fifty. Though, even *that* was petty compared to her current plan. Ashley pulled one book of accounting records from the drawer. Then, she reached into her personal black bag. Removing an identical-looking book, she switched ledgers.

Tears rimmed her clover green eyes, as she thought, *You're about to cross a federal line. No,* she disputed herself. *You're a mother, doing what you must do to survive. Someday, you'll replace this money. Someday, you'll redeem yourself.*

Unable to stand the sight of the black book, she buried it in the drawer. Looking around, an eerie quiet echoed inside her ears. She quickly maximized a digital window, signing into a bank account. The password was E-Cole-I. Clearly it wasn't her property to access.

Ashley recommended the password to her boss, flirting over drinks one night. "That name would be so cute," she teased, wiping a spot of chocolate off his lips. "I dare you to try it!" Sure enough, her charm worked.

Her legs shifted, heels jittered in anticipation. After forcing herself to press the enter button, the deposit went through. The computer left her with a message. *Thank you for doing business with us, Mr. Ethan Cole. We look forward to your next transaction.*

"Let's hope there won't be a next time," she said, exhaling.

Torn between relief and stress, she began to massage her shoulders, reclining in her seat. Another force overcame her. She looked around at the dark office, assuring everyone gone for the weekend. *Should I?* Ashley wondered. Turned on by her naughty act, something naughtier crossed her mind. *Do it.*

Throwing caution to the dogs, she opened a separate digital window. A bright screen of numbers morphed into a dark vision of bondage and sexuality. Flipping through the different scenarios, she arrived at her most cherished fantasy. Matching the thought in her mind, it showed a boss beating his employee. Bent over a desk, the curvy blonde's red cheeks were hand-spanked.

Ashley's hand roved her breasts, slowly sliding down her belly, disappearing between her skirt. Her face tensed as she felt the first drop of wetness. While one hand diddled her kitty, another unbuttoned her standard white shirt.

With each snap, her thoughts continued to flow. *Mr. Cole could come in at any moment...any employee can. Maybe he needed to tell me something...or forgot some paperwork. Instead, he'll punish me for ruining his leather seat with my juices.*

Reaching the halfway point, more buttons and thoughts were unleashed. Focusing on the spanking image, a whole new scenario entered her mind. *What if he discovered my crimes, forcing me to be his whore? He'd use and degrade me in every way possible.*

The thought of being caught had frightened her, which added to her arousal. A dose of reality went a long way into her fantasies. As her shirt was fully opened, she spread it wide.

Her face tensed, as multiple fingers entered her. Pulling down her bra, she freed one C-cup at a time. Since it wasn't unclasped, her breasts were pressed, puffing the mammaries into a pressurized mass. Squeezing each nipple, she yanked in a milking style motion.

The more her fingers pumped her, the harder she pulled at her red nubs. Ashley's fantasy darkened with each moment, as she imagined the entire office using her as punishment. Suddenly, her legs shook with spasms. A deep grunt sounded from her throat.

Her body trembled with quakes, as she bit down upon her bottom lip. The orgasm lasted a good three-minutes including aftershocks. Removing her hand, she lifted it to her face. Bringing the fingers to her nostrils, she inhaled the sweet scent.

Opening her mouth, Ashley eagerly engulfed them. Sucking every drop of syrup, she swallowed it down. She couldn't get enough, going deeper into her throat, until gagging herself. Forcing a withdrawal, her fantasy fizzled.

Someone may see you! She chastised herself, adjusting to a post-orgasm reality. Quickly fixing her underwear into place, she buttoned her shirt. With the pleasure spent, she was only left with fear and guilt. Although it fueled her fantasy, having her crimes discovered was her worst nightmare. Shutting down her computer, she quickly exited the building. *He'll never catch me...because I'll never steal from him again,* she swore to herself. Whether she believed it or not.

*****

That night, a light flashed in the dark office. A bearded man crept toward Ashley's computer. He was a private detective named Dick Martin. Ethan called him Private Dick.

Kneeling down, the man removed a concealed camera from under Ashley's desk. Next, he downloaded the hard-drive's contents. Deep inside, a secret data program recorded every word

Ashley wrote. It logged every website she visited. Unfortunately for her, it documented every transaction she made.

*****

Ashley Taylor parked in her home's driveway. She sat quietly, blankly staring at her humble abode. *Would it be wrong of me to hit the highway...and keep going?* She knew it would, though what did *that* matter? She already considered herself a bad person.

Instead, she exited the car, into the house. Ashley entered, seeing her children bounce peanuts off her husband's head. "What are you guys doing?"

"He just stares at the wall all day. Is daddy dead or just dumb?" her son asked.

"I think both," her daughter added.

"No...he just...worked hard today. Looking for a job!"

The kids looked at the wall. "You can get a job from the wall?" the boy sarcastically asked.

"Mom, is smoking pot a job?" the young girl followed.

Ashley cringed, "Where did you learn that word?"

"You. When you called him the pot smoking dickhead."

Mrs. Taylor sighed, "You weren't supposed to hear that...forget I ever said it." She truly loved the man she married. Unfortunately, *that* man vanished in a self-blazed fog. Once her motivated husband turned to legalized pot, he became an official citizen of Amsterdam. In other words, he reclined in his Lazy Boy chair all day.

"You know what...keep throwing the peanuts. In fact...let me have a shot," she said, grabbing a bowl at his side. Flinging them, the kids cheered in excitement. The noise revived him.

"You're home!" Todd said.

"Thanks for noticing. I'll start dinner...continue on, kids."

"Continue what?" he asked.

She started cooking, as the children assaulted him with flying nuts. She sighed, never expecting to be the breadwinner. Her father worked, mother stayed home raising children. Although she accepted times had changed, Ashley resented the fact she didn't have a choice. The stressed young woman resented bearing the weight of their world.

Dumping starchy noodles into a watery pot, she hopelessly watched Todd. Comfortable in his jobless malaise, he hadn't moved all day. She had to accept it. His skill and earning worth vanished. Their future was in her hands alone.

*****

After a quiet dinner, the two relaxed in bed. "Why so down tonight?" Todd asked.

"Oh, I don't know. Maybe because...I just became eligible for *federal prison*," she sarcastically answered.

"That's a reason to be high, not low...we finally did it! Three hundred-thousand reasons to be happy!"

"Or three hundred-thousand reasons not to drop the soap!" she proclaimed.

"Damn it, woman...you sure know how to kill a buzz."

"Let me get this straight. I'm robbing my company...so you can smoke more weed?"

He got quiet. "It's legal now!"

"So is showering...though you don't seem to exercise *that* right anymore! This money was for our kids' survival."

"Chill out."

"If you chilled any more...you'd be a frozen bag of peas. Just forget it," she said, turning over.

He moved in, kissing her neck. "I'll stop smoking soon...I just need some motivation."

"So you smoke something that zaps it?"

"Just trying to help."

She exhaled, turning back toward him. "Listen...I'm sorry. It's just that...even though the rent's paid, kids are fed, and savings secured...I've never been more scared in my life."

Both exhaled at the same time. "Are you sure you don't want to spark one?" he wondered.

She shot him a dirty look. "The only spark my future holds is an electric chair."

"Don't be so dramatic...they don't execute for stealing money. Just keep up the plan...everything will be fine. Flirt with him...milk the rich bastard for a few more hundred thousand."

"We agreed this was it! Don't you realize...for all we stole in the past, tonight we crossed a legal line."

"That's just legal mumbo-jumbo."

"To the woman on the front lines...it means a federal penitentiary. I really wouldn't make a good prison-bitch."

"You won't be caught! If you were, I'd take the fall...go to prison," he said unconvincingly.

"Great! That makes me feel *so* much better!" she sarcastically implied.

"Just keep working your magic," he assured, leaning in for another kiss.

She turned away. "I'm not feeling very *magical* tonight. Besides, I'm still on the rag...couple more days."

"By the way, I disagree. You'd make one hell-of-a prison-bitch! Your bunkmates would die for those juicy breasts."

She shook her head, "Great, I'll be sure to find one with tattoos and man-hands."

He touched her breasts, as she turned off the light. It was clear she was turned off as well.

*****

Friday evening arrived, as Mr. Ethan Cole sat at his desk. Joined by the private detective, they eagerly watched select clips of Ashley's actions. Illegal activity flashed across the screen.

"She hacked the company account! I knew it wasn't only a declining profit." Ethan yelled. "All along I thought she was a good girl...not a professional thief. The bottom-line was bad enough without her help."

"Don't give her so much credit. I've been at this a while...she's no pro. Someone told her the password," the detective said.

Mr. Cole got quiet.

The next clip was from the under desk camera. It recorded the ledger being switched. However, Ethan's eyes were distracted, awaiting an up-skirt.

"With legs like that...maybe she's a pro, after all," the private eye said, stopping the video feed.

"No, keep it going! I want to see it all," Mr. Cole demanded.

"Isn't that enough to prosecute?"

"I need to see the whole thing...every second."

"Oh, I get it. You want some panty action."

"How dare you! What kind of man do you think I am?"

"The *man* kind...and yeah, there's some good stuff," he said, writing down a number sequence. "The last show is a good one...here's the timeframe...you'll love it. I'll leave you to your...investigation," he mocked, exiting the room.

Left alone, Ethan cued the timeframe. Arriving at the numbers, a fantasy flashed before his eyes. Ashley's smooth legs shined, contrasting a black dress and G-string panties.

Mrs. Taylor's legs shifted into multiple positions, opening wider as time ticked on. Her heels jittered, dancing around in anticipation. The more her thighs stretched, the deeper the G-string sank into her crack.

He watched the digital window open. It was synced in time with her desk camera. Her usual financial websites were suddenly vacated, changing with her bodily demeanor.

The screen of numbers dimmed to the dark vision. Ethan's 8-inch cock grew another half. Pre-cum clogged his steamy stem. Temporarily forgetting about embezzlement, he unbuttoned his strained slacks. Lowering the pricey pants and silk boxers, he stroked himself.

His moment of fantasy was about to be extended. As Ashley's ghostly cursor clicked away, it froze upon the thumbnail. He gasped in disbelief, seeing a similar-looking boss, spanking his blond employee.

Discovering that their fantasies were shared by a touch of taboo, his strokes increased in intensity. The man's eyes nearly spewed from their sockets, as Ashley's hand secretly slid between her legs.

First, she rubbed her soft thighs, warming her touch upon sweltering skin. Her red fingernails tickled upward, hooking her sheer white G-string from an ocean of desire. Yanking the cloth aside, a fingertip teased her wilted rose petal.

Another finger joined, entrapping her clitoris. Squeezing tightly, wide circles were formed, engorging her arousal with each spin. With the cycle in motion, her opposite hand went to work.

Ashley's thighs spread further, parting pink lips like the red sea. A porcelain fingernail led the way inside, twisting and turning along the journey. Stopping halfway, she began to thrust, letting her canal slowly adapt.

With each battering, more of her finger disappeared inside. Within minutes, she was knuckle-deep. Ethan's eyes fixated upon each detail, identifying every fresh drop of vaginal rain, noticing the slightest reshaping of her vulva.

A second finger was forced inside, welcomed into the grand palace. It didn't take long for the slip and slide ride to flow. Both fingers reached their limit, buried inside her feminine flume.

Her fingers pressed upwards, teased by a gentle scraping of nails. The digitally pixelated thighs tightened in sync with Ethan's. His muscular cheeks choked his prostate. As her pace picked up, his strokes increased speed.

Although he couldn't see her expression, he imagined the beautiful blonde's face passionately pained. He couldn't see into her criminal mind, though her eyes were momentarily his. The fantasy scenario remained onscreen. The older boss mercilessly flogged his younger employee's reddened behind. The girl in the thumbnail shed tears, turning Ethan on more.

A moment of Ashley's betrayal popped into his head, threatening to kill his fantasy. Though, the more he thought of her illegal action, the more tempting reality became. *I finally have a way to live my fantasy. I can finally bring my dark desires to life!*

As the realization filled his head, spurts of sperm squirted from him. While busy soiling himself, Ashley's finale played before his eyes. In a ballet of bliss, her thighs clamped upon her fingers. Mrs. Taylor's knuckles were now fully inside her.

Vaginal flesh choked away, smothering the dual invaders of their lives. Her legs shook with spasms, forcing the high-heels to buckle. Mr. Cole couldn't hear, smell, see, touch or taste her, though all fives senses identified her essence.

Once her body calmed, the appendages were withdrawn. As she separated her fingers, clear lines of lust strung from one to the other. The proof of her pleasure disappeared from the frame, as Ethan could only imagine her tasting it.

Digital Ashley returned her G-string into place, as Ethan Cole shamefully mopped his liquid love with a wrinkled shirt.

Tucking the sticky evidence, he paused the recording. Focusing on the porn clip of a boss punishing his worker, he told himself, "This must be dealt with harshly." Since she'd never afford $300,000, it would be repaid in an entirely different way.

If I do this, there's no turning back. I'll have to keep my promises...carry out the sentence in full. She'll either serve me...or go to jail. Thinking it's the easy way out...Ashley Taylor will choose me. Unfortunately for her, prison will be a cakewalk compared to my commands.

CHAPTER TWO

Ethan angrily spent Friday night in his office. He slept on a couch, tossing and turning. His lack of sleep wasn't due to discomfort, but thoughts of being played and humiliated.

The Saturday morning dawn began to tint the shades, when a noise sounded from the building entrance. Knowing the crimes were committed after hours, mostly on weekends, Ashley's presence wasn't unexpected.

Having parked down the street, the boss's car was nowhere in sight. Ashley crept into Ethan's dark office, where she confiscated the latest spec sheets. Her eyes hadn't adjusted, while she secured them in her hands. A voice suddenly startled her. "Good morning, Mrs. Taylor."

A horrific gasp sounded from her lungs. The papers flew into the air, as her worst fear came true. "Ethan! I was just...doing a little weekend overtime."

"Quiet!" he shouted, testing a newfound empowerment she'd never heard from him. In fact, she'd never heard it from anyone. The young blond obeyed his command, almost fearful of the aggressive manner. Ethan stood, pointing to a chair facing his desk. "Take a seat." He remained standing.

"Ethan, I...I really have work to do...is this necessary?" she asked nervously.

"Sit!" he screamed. She immediately dropped into place. "And that's Mr. Cole to you. No...from now on, call me...sir."

Ashley gulped, completely surrendering to the mysterious alpha. She would've been turned on, if not petrified. "Yes, sir."

He cracked his knuckles while blurting out, "It's time to confess."

Mrs. Taylor's blood pressure increased 100 BPM, fighting to keep calm. "Umm...the coffee. Silly me, I changed brands without telling you...let me get you a cup. I know you'll love it," she said, rushing to pour the liquid. Her hand trembled, clinking the cold glass pot against his porcelain mug.

"We both know this isn't a matter of caffeine. It's one of criminality. You've been stealing from me."

Her hand stopped pouring, though the clinking clamored on. She placed the cup on his desk, trying to think of an excuse. "Petty cash...I needed gas money...took a couple of bucks...I'm sorry," she said. "Dock my pay...we can overlook this, can't we? I'll work overtime as punishment."

He slammed his hand on the desk's surface. Momentarily shuddering, the attractive girl's power was gone, beauty neutralized.

Held captive by his manly rage, her plastic moat of strength crumbled. "Damn it! You know we've had a major tax increase recently...one you used to your advantage. The least you could do is admit your betrayal."

Her head sank, eyes welled with water. "I'm sorry." She broke down. Hating to cry in front of men, she feared jail even more. As real as the tears were, the high school drama star worked her emotions.

"At least, that's a start," he said, appearing to soften.

Dropping to her knees, she begged, "You're right. I know we have financial problems...but mine are worse. My husband's been unemployed for a year...we're broke." She placed a hand upon his.

For a moment, he almost felt pity. Then, he remembered all her flirty compliments and back rubs. *Lies!* He bitterly told himself. Yanking his hand away, he declared, "The Robin Hood excuse won't matter to the police."

Her tears turned to sobs. "Please.... please don't send me to jail! I'll do anything...anything you tell me."

Ethan's eyebrows rose, empowered by mere words. Ignored by girls throughout his school years, cruel tricks and teases haunted him to the current day. Ashley would pay the price for them all.

"You have until tomorrow to turn yourself in. I'll give you a chance to tell your husband...get your affairs in order. If not, I'll call the authorities myself."

Mrs. Taylor trembled, smearing a line of wet mascara from her eyes. *You knew this was coming, face it.* The frightened girl stood upon her heels, teetering like a newborn giraffe. "My husband had nothing to do with this...please don't press charges on him," she said. "Someone has to raise my young kids."

I forgot about her kids. Having a young child of his own, guilt choked him. Though, his ex-wife quickly changed that. Haunting his thoughts, he remembered her denying visitation rights, while taking his child support. Gazing down into his cup of coffee, a bitter man stared back.

The time to offer his deal had come. He circled her, like a rapid mutt ready to bite. She dropped to her knees, breaking the tense silence. "Beat me if you have to...anything to spare me from jail!"

Shaking with fury, he grabbed her by the elbows. Her limp body was dragged towards the desk, flung onto the oak surface. As she landed, her legs flew into the air. Exposed to him, she studied the rage upon his face. He approached her like a snarling beast.

Her one-piece dress was fastened by a hemline of centered buttons. Each one popped off, as he tore it downward. The curvy blond gasped in fright. He cruelly snapped her C-cup bra upon the throbbing mammaries. A set of hard nipples nearly pierced the unpadded, white cloth. The man's angry hands yanked her bra overhead, never unclasping it.

As her milky-white breasts flopped out, they jiggled in the roughhousing. He slapped at each one, continuing their motion. Ashley's hands grabbed hold of the desk's edge, fighting the stinging sensation. Using every ounce of anger and strength, he forced her panties down.

Realizing what was happening, her thighs quickly closed in defense. "I'm on my period!" she begged. "It's almost over...in two days...it'll be gone. You can do it then!"

The disgust in her eyes only enticed him more. Without speaking a word, he forced her legs into a split, tearing her sheer white G-string at the crotch. Digging his fingers into the tear, he finished the job. Ripping outward, the flimsy cloth shred like recycled paper. Her hips were stretched so wide, the outer-band snapped.

As the panties fell, he flipped her on her stomach. Bent over Ethan's desk, Mrs. Taylor's round butt cheeks were fully exposed. In the first act of his mentally developed drama, he reached for a wooden yardstick.

His action caused her to gasp. *It's just like my fantasy...how'd he know? Oh shit, this is actually gonna hurt. In my head, I was in control. As scared, as I am...how is it possible I'm so wet!*

Pressing her arched back, Ashley's breasts were squashed into the desk. Ethan's arm cracked backward in a pitching motion. His pent-up anger unleashed a swift, hard blow. Spanking her bubbly cheeks, a whipping sound filled the air. A feminine moan sounded, as the wooden whip stung her skin.

Repeating the motion, Mr. Cole hurled another whack. The crackling of skin echoed off the walls. Red lines formed upon her hind globes. Every inch of her curved crevice was punished, getting harder with each administering.

Tears spilled from Ashley's eyes, draining more mascara with it. However, the tears weren't only from pain. The act unleashed a submission she hadn't felt since childhood. Over the years, her beauty formed a shallow casing of strength. As that barrier was penetrated, it shattered, leaving her vulnerable and exposed.

The harder she cried, the worthier Ethan felt. They had traded places. As Ashley got weaker, Mr. Cole became mentally and physically stronger.

Suddenly, Ashley's shaking legs gave out, causing her to fall upon her knees. Forming a human ball, she expected a moment of mercy. There was none offered. Instead, he leaned inward to her. "Of the thousands of dollars you'll work off...you've just earned one."

Returning her into position, he went to flog her again. Suddenly, he paused in wonderment. With every ruler blow, Ashley had tightened, tensed, and pushed. Although she mentioned her menstrual condition earlier, the visual aroused his sickest fantasy.

Dropping the ruler, he spread her weak legs further. Reaching in between, Ethan gripped the dangling white string from her vaginal lips. Yanking it out, he tossed the red tampon aside.

Another gasp sounded from Ashley's lungs. She'd never felt more humiliated in her life. By the time she could even comprehend Ethan's plans, Mrs. Taylor was flipped onto her back again.

"Please...don't do this," she begged.

As Mr. Cole studied her embarrassed face, he noticed it was as red as her vaginal lips. *The less she wants it...the more she'll get it,* he told himself. *That's what punishment is all about.*

Unzipping his pants, his bulging 8-inch cock popped out. She was shocked, used to her husband's thin 5-inches. Even though she'd had plenty of sexual partners, she'd never been in less control of the situation.

Ethan pulled the smooth legs towards him, sliding her curved buns to the desk's edge. Already soaked with bodily fluids, the boss's arrow struck Ashley's bullseye. Offering little ease, his veined villain invaded her most private area, at its most private time.

As slick as she was, her vaginal limits were tested. Slipping fully inside her, the rough ramming began. With every outward stroke, a crimson covering shellacked Ethan's penis with cherry-vanilla stain.

Ashley cringed in a chorus of pain, pleasure, and personal disgust. Shame filled every inch of her, as a sopping ocean trickled through her anal creek. Having never had menstrual sex, she'd always shied away from the barbarous act.

She shielded her eyes, when a morbid curiosity suddenly claimed her. Her hidden dark-side emerged, aching to see the taboo sight. She snuck a peek. Straining her neck, a pair of clover green eyes watched Ethan's hammer crack her cobbler.

Ashley's high-heels tensed upon the man's squared shoulders. Her vaginal canal expanded, officially relinquishing her queendom, crowning him king. The more she watched the naturally barbaric act unfold, a primal urge filled her. Her long blond hair spilled off the glossy desk's edge. Shutting her eyes, she accepted every inch of him.

An act, which once disgusted her, enhanced the moment. She was officially conquered, taken by animalistic force like a cavewoman. The only tool missing from the experience was a wooden club, used to knock her out.

Her fluids began to fiercely flow, making squashing sounds upon impact. Sprays of slush splattered out, emulating boots in fresh rain puddles. Pale white skin was dotted with a sprinkling of crimson desire.

As vaginal pressure began to build, an orgasm simmered inside the depths of her soul. Her face tightened in fits of lust. As Ashley's inner muscles began to choke the spear, Ethan quickly withdrew.

Like a shaken bottle of Champaign, Mrs. Taylor's orgasm remained corked. Instead, her boss spun her around like a wheel of misfortune. "You'll cum when I give you permission," he said, stroking his glazed kebob over her face. She tried to turn away, held forcefully by a hand upon her neck.

Within moments, a river of slippery seed drowned her face. Gritty grunts escaped Ethan's throat, unleashing a river of pent up justice. Ashley tried to keep her mouth shut, though his grasp shifted to deny her nostrils of air.

As her nose was pinched shut, Ashley's mouth was forced open. A heavy stream filled her cavity, overshooting her cheeks. Her throat could barely contain the quickly draining offering. Seeing it escape, he pinned her exit shut, forcing her to swallow his swirling statement. She ingested his authority.

Upon the boss's finish, Mrs. Taylor attempted to clean the facemask of manly mud. He stopped the action. "Leave it...as a message for your husband. You're mine now. It will be a reminder that no one in this goes unpunished. It will also be an appropriate last sight to remember you by."

Tears rimmed her humiliated eyes, as she hopped off the desk. "Last sight? I have to live with you? How long will this haunt me for?"

"How long have you been stealing from me?"

She looked away, hiding her cum covered face, red stained thighs. "A few months."

"Bullshit! One year...you're my property," he demanded. "You've been stealing since the day I hired you. Whether my money...or self-respect. You'll earn every cent back."

"What happens if I quit...run away?"

"I'll dedicate my life to finding you. Take my word for it...the courts will sentence you longer than a year. It's up to you...feel free to stop at any time. If you choose to accept, consider the contract signed in blood...the menstrual kind."

She gasped in distress. "Are you really going to keep me prisoner?"

"Take the extended weekend...spend time with your kids, husband...tell them goodbye. Although Monday's a vacation day, your work officially begins."

She shook in disbelief, reaching down for her panties. There was nothing left to salvage. Tossing the rags aside, she grabbed her white dress.

"Wait one minute," he announced.

"More? Haven't you done enough for today?"

He looked over at the Xerox machine. "Come here," he ordered, taking hold of her arm. Securing her hips in his hands, he lifted her to the long bed of glass. The dress dropped to the floor, as she was sprawled upon her smooth stomach. Each nipple was pressed into the cold slab, along with her messed slit.

"Why are you making me do this? What purpose will it serve?"

"You'll find out...when I want you to," he said. After cueing the electronic machine, a blinding light haloed her body. Landing in a copy bin, one sheet of paper followed another. Ethan examined the work of modern art. A womanly display of breasts and vagina were clearly shown, stains included.

As the copies finished, he secured them inside a locked drawer. Lifting her off the machine, she scrambled for her dress again. Since the buttons were torn off, she could only hide her exposed vanity by tightly shrouding it. A red stain immediately soaked through the thin material, bringing her more shame. "I'm beginning to think jail might be easier."

"The option's still there. Think it over now...because it's only the beginning."

*****

Crying all the way home, Ashley pulled her Ford Focus into the driveway. She exited the car in haste, wrapping her dress tight. In the height of daylight, any neighbor would've gotten a peep show. Luckily for her, none were out. However, there was one presence she pretended to ignore.

The disgraced woman sprinted to her front door, as a Mercedes Benz waited in front of the house. The window slowly rolled down, ensuring Ethan could hear every word spoken.

Fumbling her keys, a honk quickly interrupted Ashley's action. She gasped, dropping the keys. Before she could retrieve them, her stoned husband opened the door. He was shocked by his half-nude, cum-covered wife. Breaking down in tears, she rushed past him.

Todd looked out at the car, seeing a dark-haired stranger wave back. Although he'd never seen the man, there was no doubt who he was. One last honk sounded, as Mr. Cole drove away.

The stunned and stoned Mr. Taylor watched in disbelief. He was afraid to face his wife for many reasons. *Am I busted? Am I going to jail...for smoking and growing? Oh wait, it's legal now.* He sounded a dopey giggle, laughing at his own joke. *Was my wife really covered in cum...or did I smoke some really bad weed? Is this all a hallucination?* There was one fact he didn't have to inquire about.

Yeah, we're fucked.

CHAPTER THREE

"I can't believe you came home with a cum face," the stoned Todd Taylor said, lying in bed with his wife.

A mortified Ashley shot him a look of disbelief. "Let me get this straight. I was beaten with a yardstick, forced to have bloody sex, could go to prison for years...and *that's* what's on your mind?"

"Was that insensitive? Sorry. It's just...how can I kiss you from now on?"

"Whoever said legalizing pot was a good idea...is truly an asshole!" She turned over in a huff.

"You really have to live there for a whole year?"

She turned back over in anger. "No. There's always a barred cell and bearded girlfriend named Chris," she sarcastically said. "Of course I have to. Mr. Cole gave me the deal...I have to accept it!"

"When do you go?"

"Monday."

"Will he at least let you come home to cook for me? And who's gonna change the kid's diapers?"

"The kids are 6 and 7...they don't wear diapers anymore! Please tell me you haven't lost *that* many brain cells?"

He giggled again, "Sorry, I experimented with a new strain tonight...damn strong. We'll get by. Hell, maybe the kids and I will bond."

"That bond better not include smoke!"

"Nothing but a camp fire!"

Ashley flipped back over. "I don't even want to think about it. If you would've only seen the anger in Ethan's eyes."

"Well, I guess you can't blame the man."

"Excuse me?"

"You stole a fortune from him. If you include petty cash, you took from everyone there. I'd probably have done worse than he did."

"*WE* stole that money. In fact, I remember it being your bright idea...Mr. Dickweed!"

"I said *we*...didn't I?"

Ignoring him, she turned off the light. A few moments of silence sounded, as Todd began snoring. For a moment, she smiled, thinking, *I'll miss my kids. As wasted as he his...I'll even miss Todd...maybe.* However, one thought outweighed them all. *Come Monday...my life is no longer mine.*

*****

Monday arrived, as Ethan announced, "You touch nothing without asking, understand?"

She nodded, nervously entering his home. Gazing around, Ashley marveled at a large great room, wanting to compliment it. However, she quickly remembered it wasn't a stay of pleasure, but punishment. "Where will I sleep?" she asked.

"Follow me," he said, leading her down a hallway of rooms. Passing each one, the doors were slightly open. Massive feather beds were dwarfed by cathedral ceilings. Seventy-inch flat-screens adorned the walls, featuring every national and international channel.

Maybe this won't be so bad, like a spa vacation, she silently thought. *That* fantasy ended, as they arrived at the hall's end room. The door opened, revealing a walk-in closet. "Is this where I'll store my things?" she asked.

"No, this is where I'll store *my* thing...as in...*you*," he informed. "This is your room." There was no window, TV, pictures, or mattress. Her bedding was a blanket on the floor with a flat pillow.

She quickly reminded herself, *Remember, you were prepared for anything. It could be much worse.*

"Looks very comfortable," she said, refusing to show weakness.

"Good, because you'll spend a lot of time here. The hallway provides ambient light during the day. After sundown...it gets dark," he said with a smirk.

"No light?" she asked in an upsetting manner. Quickly returning to her plan, she took a breath. "That'll be fine. What now?"

He momentarily exited the room. She began to unpack, realizing there were no drawers to put her things. Then she remembered she wouldn't need those things anyway.

He returned with two hands behind his back. Ashley gasped, thinking, *What sick, sexual act will he perform this time? Electrocution? Decapitation? Whatever it is...it will be extreme, sadistic, shocking, and sexual.*

"For you," he said, unveiling a maid uniform and feather duster.

"Are you serious? I'm a *maid*?"

"Don't worry, it won't be your main job."

She snatched it from his hands.

"You're to clean the house, top to bottom...daily. Every floor will be vacuumed, shelf dusted, and toilet scrubbed. After that, you'll prepare for our guests," he said, exiting the room.

Mrs. Taylor gazed down at her maid outfit. It was the classic black uniform with a sexier, shorter cut. Bitterly pulling off her clothes, she put on the uniform. It came with matching thigh-high stockings, no shoes or panties. She decided to leave her white thong on. *Maybe he won't even notice,* she unconvincingly thought.

She entered the great room, performing her first cleaning. Ethan Cole sat back, watching his servant work. Reaching for a low spot, she bent over, revealing her riding thong.

Before she returned to an upright position, a pair of hands trapped her hips. Twisting the bands of her thong around his fingers, he broke the bands with one snap. They fell to her feet. "You will never wear panties in this house again. Do you understand?"

"Yes, sir."

Ethan returned to his seat, as Ashley stepped out of the white panty ring. Finishing the pool table, she moved to a mysterious black stool. It resembled a saddle from a bull-riding machine. The particular one was propped up by four legs.

"Does this need to be cleaned too?"

"Yes."

"Do you mind if I ask what it is?"

"Yes, I mind." He remained silent.

She bent over again, dusting the black leather. As she did, her curved ass cheeks formed a heart shape. Her slit was pressed together, creating an inviting target. However, Ethan wanted to keep her fresh for later. It would be rude to introduce her to new guests while smelling of cum.

He followed her around the entire house, watching her scrub on her hands and knees. His cock grew harder with every different position she took. By the end of 4000 square feet, she'd formed them all.

"I'm done," she said, wiping sweat from her brow.

"Take a shower...clean your vagina well. You're to change into a new outfit for the guests. It's in your room."

After scrubbing herself clean, she entered her quarters to find a sheer body stocking. As she stretched it over her seams, it snapped into place, fitting snuggly. The see-through teaser hugged every curve, netting her nipples like fresh catch.

She ran her hands across the deadly slopes. Each one was enhanced by the sexy outfit, sure to get the mysterious guests hot. She continued to wonder who they were or what they'd do to her.

That all changed when the doorbell sounded. She gasped, preparing herself for the unknown. Heading for the door, the sound of four male voices filled her ears.

*****

Taking her hand, Mr. Cole led Ashley into the great room. Three strangers sat upon the couch, featuring blond, black, and brunette hair. All of them were unknown to her, which calmed her. *At least they're not from work. I'd be so humiliated by people I knew.*

Brought to the mysterious stool, her attention was distracted by an electronic flash. Studying the 85-inch flat screen, Ashley was suddenly the star of the show. So was the black box. Gazing downward, she acknowledged a new addition. A long, plastic dildo was attached to the machine's surface.

Mr. Cole stepped up to the crowd. Although there was no formal introduction, she was announced. "I promised you boys an experience you'll never forget. We'll start...with a rodeo show. We'll start with a Sybian!"

Having heard of it from porn, the males' mouths watered. Familiar with a rodeo, they were clearly not Ethan's usual friends. Instead, he found them at a bar, catcalling the bull-riding victims. "Put her on it now!" the drunk blond man yelled.

"You heard the audience," Mr. Cole ordered.

"Dry?" she asked. "No lube?"

He looked over at the three young men, "Would you like to provide some...assistance?"

After looking at each other, they hurried over. Each one spit upon the long knob, creating a human slide of slipperiness.

Ashley gasped, silently saying, *Next time, just keep your mouth shut!* Having no choice, she straddled the round black machine. The body stocking had an open slit at the crotch, spreading in conjunction with her thighs. Lining up her hole to the dong, she squatted. Her swollen lips made contact, attracted to the sticky plastic like a magnet.

Wrapping themselves around the pleasure pole, the lips embraced it like shrink-wrap. Sinking down, she filled her vaginal canal, landing at the beveled base. A tiny nub greeted her anus, gently pressing up against it.

"Turn it on!" the men yelled. "Ride already, damn it!"

Taking a handheld remote, Ethan activated the machine. A slow buzz kick started the ride, letting the phallus slowly spin inside her. Ashley immediately tensed, feeling an array of sensations.

Mr. Cole didn't wait for a warm up. Instead, he quickly increased the machine's intensity. By the time it hit level five, the stone floor nearly cracked. The entire machine let off pulsing vibrations. Her clit buzzed like Africanized bees, as the submerged dong spun like teacups at Disney.

The men rose from the couch, cheering her on like Monday night football. They sucked bottles of Ethan's imported beer, watching Mrs. Taylor ride the reckless beast. There came a point every single nerve was stimulated inside her.

No longer able to deny it, she finally let go. Gravity took complete control. Sinking downward, her hosed thighs stuck to the black leather. Leaning forward, her clit auditioned the perfect spot. Her curved hips began spinning in small circles, alternating pressure between her vaginal and anal fault-lines.

As her feet slowly lifted off the ground, Ashley's vagina bared the full-weight of her body. Gripping the Sybian's curved edge, she rode like Ty Murray in drag. Forgetting about her audience, a moan escaped her. Electrified pulses sailed from her brain to the soles of her feet.

Suddenly remembering the camera, she opened her eyes. Staring over at the TV, the curvaceous kitten felt like a porn star. Having always loved attention, being objectified wasn't really a bad thing to her. It was her choice in the matter, which still aroused her anger. Though, even *that* fact was starting to fade.

Mesmerized by the sights, feelings, and cheers, she was about to break. Ethan was so entranced; he almost let it happen. Though, he wasn't ready to give permission yet. Her face tensed, bottom lip nearly bled, and fireworks started popping. That's when the machine stopped.

"What the hell?" the men yelled.

The shocked girl finally felt the weight of his power. Oddly enough, she also started to respect it. *He owns me,* she self-admitted. Stopping her pleasure was more satisfactory to him than administering it.

Shaking with spasms, Ashley tried to let her body calm. She was interrupted by the blond man, yelling, "Oh, hell no! She was about to finish!"

"I could let her finish...or...I could let her finish you guys. Your choice."

"Well...duh!" the three simultaneously shouted.

Mr. Cole smirked, lifting Ashley off the Sybian. Placing her upright, she could barely stand. Addressing the three men, he said, "Remove your pants."

The straight men looked at each other in suspicious wonder. "I won't look if you don't," the blond man said.

"Deal," the other two concluded.

They yanked down their jeans, revealing oozing cocks. They were thick, strained with veins, and ranged between 6-8 inches.

The boss led his employee to the blond man. "On your knees," he ordered, leading the weak girl down. Having no energy to fight, she landed at his penis. Ethan stopped her from sucking. "Since this is a night of sport...let the games continue."

Removing his leather belt, he pulled Ashley's hands behind her back. Ethan wrapped the leather strap around her wrists. Buckled in, she was tightly bound. "Now...you may begin," he said, pushing her towards the blond man's slicked cock.

Her full lips embraced the bulbous head. She began to slowly ease down, when she lost her balance. The stranger's thick cock disappeared inside her. Ashley was immediately impaled, falling into a deep-throating action.

The man moaned in pleasure. He grabbed ahold of her hair, attempting to pull her up.

"No," Ethan ordered. "Let her earn it."

"You heard him, earn it!" the blond man teased, placing his hands behind his head. She gagged again, driven even deeper into his cock. His thickness choked her. Knowing she had to think fast, Ashley placed her breasts upon the man's knees. Thrusting upward, she freed her throat.

After falling down a few more times, she used her trembling thighs to rise. Slowly, Mrs. Taylor gained muscle control. Feeling her strained, netted nipples against his knees, the man spread his legs further. Her soft body fell into him. As her breasts brushed his testicles, something wasn't right.

Deciding to take over, he freed his cock from her mouth. A dangling of saliva remained, as she looked up at him. In a hormonal rage, he tore her body stocking. Shredding the sheer fabric, one full breast spilled out. Repeating the action, the other was freed.

Already slicked with her natural juices, the man forced her breasts closer to his cock. Trapping his hardness within her bountiful blossoms, he squeezed his offering between the assets.

Ashley moaned, feeling the pressure grow. Her breasts were pushed to the bursting point, thrust up and down in a titty-fuck. Continuing to pump away, he wasn't about to let a good load go to waste. She was returned to his cock, impaled again.

The bound beauty sucked the raging rod. Since her throat was already primed, she was able to take every inch. He gripped a full head of hair. After a few more pumps, he fired buckets of sperm inside her warm-hole.

Crates of cream seeped from her lips, forcing her to furiously swallow. Noticing *that* fact, Mr. Cole gave the command. "Next!"

he ordered. Disconnected from one penis, she was slid to the second, aimed right at his offering.

Not yet empty of the last participant's filling, the dark haired man's arrow was ingested. The leftover load streaked his cock. It was only a matter of time before she cleaned it of all remnants.

Like a pecking hen, she continued the job. It didn't take long for him to leave his own load, pre-slicked by his friend. Awash in DNA, Ashley was forced onto the last man. By the time he came, her mouth and lips were drenched with cum.

Yanking her off the line, Ethan said, "Open up." She stuck out her tongue, revealing the remnants. "Swallow!"

Obeying him, she swallowed, re-opening for inspection.

"You are free to go now," he told his satisfied guests.

They yanked up their pants, as the blond man said, "Man...I don't know who you are...but I sure as hell like your style."

Mr. Cole smiled, having never been one of the boys. Ethan was certainly never leader of the pack. *A man can get used to this admiration,* he silently told himself. Of course, his newfound confidence would only last as long as Ashley's captivity.

*****

That night, Ashley reflected inside her small space, trying to make sense of her performance. The act just didn't seem real to a girl like her. In college, she'd had a few men in one night, though never in a row. Wrapping herself tightly in the blanket, Mrs. Taylor tried to adjust to the floor. *At least...it wasn't at work,* she told herself.

43

However, the workweek was about to begin. *Tuesday was the real test.*

CHAPTER FOUR

Tuesday morning arrived, as quiet filled the small office. Ashley crept inside, starting to have hope. *He might keep our secret behind the walls of his home.* Relief filled her, though oddly a streak of disappointment did too. As embarrassed, as she would've been, the fantasy was always a dark wish of hers.

That all changed as she walked by four of her coworkers. There were three males, one female. "Morning guys," she said. They didn't respond. Instead, their eyes remained glued to the computers.

Mrs. Taylor's heart rate increased, as she headed for her office. Once inside, the outer-gossip began. Peeking from her office, indecipherable whispers teased Ashley's ears. Each worker held a sheet of thin paper.

"Shhh!" the female worker announced. Spotting the spy, they quickly returned to their work.

What could they be reading...oh shit! She thought. Gazing over at her monitor, the same paper was taped to it. The trembling woman hoped it wasn't what she thought. However, she was no fool.

Examining it, her fantasy quickly merged with the nightmare. As the paper trembled in her hands, she inhaled the Xeroxed breasts and vagina. The image wasn't the worst part. It was the name above: *Meet Ashley Taylor.*

She gasped, as her mind was officially made up. The criminal was ready to turn herself in. Ashley began to approach the door, when her children's young faces flashed inside her head. Imagining the many years she'd miss of their lives, her march was halted. *You can take a year of this...no matter what they throw at you!*

A knock sounded on the door, as *that* year was about to begin. Ethan appeared. "Mrs. Taylor...please join us for a team meeting...in the conference room," he said, quickly exiting.

*****

Ashley nervously entered the conference room. As she entered, another hush filled the air. Refusing to make eye contact, she rushed for her usual seat. Ethan's hand quickly stopped her. "Not today," he said, keeping her front and center.

Seven eager people surrounded the table. The three males and a female were already there. The males had dark hair. Two wore sideburns, another a goatee. One was 18, the other two aged 20, in prime shape. The female had coffee-colored black hair with a thin body frame.

Next to them were two average-looking, male stockholders. They represented ten other shareholders, who totaled 49% of the company's ownership. The other 51% belonged to Ethan, the company's president. Seated next to them was the company VP, who was 65 years old with a shiny bald head. Confusion painted his face.

Mr. Cole held Ashley's arm tightly, while making an announcement. "Many of you have already met Mrs. Taylor...though today, you'll sadly see...you didn't know her at all."

Everyone was puzzled, having worked with the pleasant woman for a year. The vice president asked, "Excuse me, Ethan...what's *this* about?" he asked, holding up the nude copy, examining it with his glasses. "And what are those dark stains around the thighs?"

"Let me explain. You all know our financial troubles...having lived it over the last year. Having been denied a year-end raise and Christmas bonus, only to get a heavier work load...I'd bet you'd like to know why."

"You can say that again," the VP said, as everyone eagerly nodded.

"While you cut back on your personal luxuries, Mrs. Taylor went on a spree."

"That's not true!"

He gave her a dirty look, as she quieted down. "Tell them just how luxurious your life's been recently." She refused to speak. "Jail it is..."

"Wait!" she interrupted. "I stole $300,000."

A series of gasps filled the room. From the lowest paid workers to the highest stockholders, each one already suffered from a new government sin tax. However, Ashley's creative accounting pushed them over the edge. It sent the budget into havoc. Any sympathy they would've granted her, vanished with her words.

"You're not pressing charges?" The VP asked.

"I am...though not in the traditional way."

"I don't understand?"

"You see...if she goes to jail...our profit is still lost. Essentially, we gain nothing...she just loses. So, I had another idea."

Each person waited anxiously, as the VP shouted, "This better be good!"

Ethan announced, "Mrs. Taylor, serve your coworkers some coffee."

She paused, surprised by the tame suggestion. So was everyone else in the room.

"Not exactly what I had in mind," the VP said.

"Do it," Ethan demanded.

"Yes, sir." She quickly ran to the room's coffee station, beginning to pour seven cups.

"This is what we get?" A stockholder asked. "Not near the value of my plummeting shares."

Ethan remained quiet, watching her fill the cups. She grabbed one, heading to deliver it. "Nude," Mr. Cole shouted.

She stopped in mid-flight, as all eyes dashed open. "Don't do this...not here!"

"You have ten-seconds. Nine...eight...seven..."

Hearing the numbers descend, Ashley put down the cup. Her face grimaced, as she begrudgingly slipped off her one-piece red dress, giving the room a live show. Every mouth hung open, every cock rose in anticipation, equaling the lone female's nipple intensity. The girl wasn't as innocent as she looked.

As the dress hit the floor, Mrs. Taylor's bra was unsnapped, unleashing her pillowy breasts. She wrapped her thumbs around her thong panties, held up by tied strings. Hesitating at her heavenly hips, Ethan emphasized his current number. "TWO..."

Untying the strings like a wrapped gift's bow, the panties fell to the floor. After kicking off her heels, she cupped her breasts and vagina. Her bashful expression pointed downward. "She can't deliver my coffee while holding those moon pies," the VP shouted.

"One," Ethan finished. "You heard the man...deliver the coffee."

After a deep exhale, she turned around. Heading toward the cups, her curved ass swayed with each step. All eyes remained on the perfect hourglass, watching Ashley's sensual sands spill.

Grabbing two cups of coffee, she turned, revealing her triangle of temptation. Her teardrop breasts bounced in beautiful rhythm. She set the first cup down at the vice president, nearly piercing his eye with her aroused nipples.

As she leaned over the table, the VP's aggressive hand traced her curved backside. He ended with a firm slap. Having received much harder, Ashley remained calm. She went to grab the other cups, as an idea struck Ethan. *If spanking her helped me burn some anger, it will help them too.*

He stopped her again, re-addressing his workers. "I think we can do better than coffee. In fact, I know it," he said, bending her over the conference table. "Tell me what you want from her.

Remember, this is your yearly raise, bonus, and vacation...make it count."

His words made the undervalued staff's blood boil. "Spankings...to start!" the VP insisted.

Ethan nodded. "We'll begin each morning with it...let off steam. Form a line."

Ashley gasped, seeing all seven line up. To ensure she didn't squirm, Mr. Cole pressed her body against the table, nearly flattening her breasts. He held her arms down, noticing her tampon string was gone. Disappointment filled him.

One of the three lower employees took the first spot. Having never done it before, he looked down at his open hand, then back at Ethan. "As hard as you want."

The young man gazed at the target. In his eyes, there might as well been a bullseye on the roast-worthy rump. The position enhanced every buttock curve, forming a tight tarp. Ashley never felt so vulnerable in her life.

A sharp spank sounded, brandished by the spirit of youth. As Mrs. Taylor moaned, a large smile crossed the male's face. He felt the sting, realizing that her sensitive behind hurt even more.

Another spanking was administered, followed by a succession of fury. Red handprints covered one generalized area, receiving the most punishment. He continued until his hand tired of energy.

"Next," Ethan said, as another young coworker stepped up. One by one, the line lessened, leaving her bountiful cheeks bludgeoned. With each new beating, Ashley's feminine feet were stretched off the ground, using her toes to prop her.

She didn't think she could take anymore, when the last employee stepped up. The thin, brunette female took a different approach. While the men got off on the cruelty, she tapped into a natural compassion.

A gentle feminine hand touched the hot redness, making Ashley jolt in fear. The girl assured her, "I'm not gonna hurt you." Her smooth hand gently soothed sore skin. A tender rubbing calmed the pain, cooled by a pair of translucent fingernails.

Chills began to cover Mrs. Taylor's body, when a surprise spanking was unleashed. It wasn't hard, but firm. The thin brunette switched between the light spankings and tickling touches...toying with all emotions. Within moments, a gentle shudder danced across Ashley's porcelain skin.

The real shock belonged to Ethan. He'd never imagined she'd orgasm from such a simple act. For a moment, he even questioned his own methods. He then remembered his job was to punish, not pleasure.

His thoughts were interrupted by the company vice president. "You call *that* a bonus?"

"Our portfolios barely budged!" the stockholders demanded.

"It was no vacation!" the three males said, with the female remaining silent on the matter.

"Who said we were finished? I told you...she's yours to do what you want. Whatever you desire, for a full year. Make a wish, it will be granted."

"I want something she'll never forget!" the VP insisted. "Most people would do hard time for her crime!"

"I'm waiting for suggestions," Ethan said.

A pause filled the room, though everyone knew what was on the joint male mind. "Sex!" they all yelled out, minus two voices.

The brunette girl's non-response was expected. However, the VP unleashed a hidden streak of sadism. "When I was a kid...punishments were more symbolic than spankings. It was about purging someone of their sin...cleaning them out."

Ethan smirked, "Clean her out? A bar of soap...in her mouth?"

The VP paused, staring down at the cup of cooled, black coffee. "Not soap...and not her mouth."

"Vaginal enema?" Mr. Cole asked. "Coffee?"

"It's quite common these days...and safe, minus a little caffeine kick. You gave us all a choice. They made theirs...that's mine."

"We...we don't even have the equipment," Mr. Cole insisted, trying to avoid the mess.

The enthused VP ran towards the bottled water dispenser. Grabbing a handful of cylinder shaped cups, he took a coffee stirrer, perforating the bottom point. "All you need now is a pot of coffee...and a bad girl."

A fearful Mrs. Taylor looked back at Ethan, who turned his gaze away from her. "Go ahead."

Gasps of shock sounded, as the 65 year-old man approached the nude woman. He pulled Ashley to her feet. Spinning her around, his hands lifted the helpless blond onto the table. Pushing her onto her back, he lifted her knees into a stirrup-like position.

Eagerly spreading Ashley's soaking lips, the bald VP extended his tongue, lapping up the feminine honey. After swallowing the sweet treat, he deposited some natural fluid, prepping her with homemade lubricant.

The cupped funnel was eased into her spread hole. "Give me the pot," he shouted, like a mad scientist to an assistant. Ethan grabbed it, assuring it was cooled first. Panic filled Ashley, as her airborne legs jittered. The coffee was poured into the jury-rigged funnel.

Mrs. Taylor wiggled like a snake bitten horse, spilling the high-end coffee all over them. "Damn it! This isn't going to work." The VP looked around, focusing on his necktie. He yanked the solid red rag from his body. "Everyone, follow my lead."

Apprehensive, yet curious, the men removed their ties. Stretching Ashley's arms outward, her wrists were individually knotted. Joining a few together, the line of ties was secured to conference chairs. Returning her legs into an upright position, the appendages were also roped into place.

The captive woman instinctively tried to free herself, though the heavy oak chairs barely budged. "She'll hold," the VP proclaimed.

With three neckties remaining, her eyes were blindfolded to calm any fear. Her mouth was deeply gagged, just in case she screamed. The last tie was wrapped around her mouth. Since they shared a building with others, no noises could be chanced. As the cylinder was returned into place, the VP took initiative.

The paper cylinders were fitted deeper inside her vaginal canal. Unable to escape, Ashley's body finally went limp. Having no sight of the coming invasion, she awaited the cold surprise.

An aroma of roasted beans filled the air, as a faucet of darkness spun into the funnel. A swirling whirl of coal-colored liquid filled her tender tube. Ashley's body jolted to life, shocked by the invigoration.

Confusion filled her brain, as the caffeinated invader stretched her canal. Mrs. Taylor's toes tightened into small balls, spinning with stress. The harder she pulled at her silk restraints, the quicker and deeper the liquid penetrated.

The glass pot emptied. As her pink palace filled, the coffee trickled through her cervix into her uterus. Feeling the strange sensation, Ashley flailed her captive arms. Each of the four oak chairs swayed in opposite timing. Fresh out of ammo, the VP called for the remaining cups.

His eager audience ran for their share, handing them to him. *Will she explode?* They all wondered, as more cups were dumped, letting heavy liquid swell upon her G-spot.

By the last one, the VP shouted, "Untie her!" Ethan grabbed one side; a stockholder freed the other. Mrs. Taylor's buttery thighs were forced together, sealing the enema in.

Her ankles were bound, assuring she couldn't break them. Although she grunted through her gag, it was useless. No words were decipherable, and no one would've listened if they were.

"How long?" Ethan asked.

"Keep watching," the VP answered, studying the tightening expression.

And I thought I was a sick bastard, Mr. Cole silently thought. *He's obviously done this before.*

Five minutes dragged by, as Ashley's tummy was partially puffed. As she continued to writhe around in cramps, her clamped thighs struggled to retain the bulging liquid. "What are we waiting for exactly?" Ethan asked.

"This," the VP said, dropping to his knees.

The gagged girl bit down on the thick cloth. She shook with shudders, exploding in a different way than expected. Chills crawled through her body, tingling every nerve from head to toe.

Seeing his opportunity, the VP untied Ashley's legs. With her lips already at the table's edge, he leaned downward, spreading her wide open. A stream of warm coffee exited her vagina, slowly filling his mouth. Everyone watched in disturbed curiosity, as she dispensed.

Her body absorbed half of it, only expelling the other half. As the stream slowed to a crawl, the thirsty VP placed his lips to hers. Sucking the liquid gold like a pipeline in an earthly crater, he cleaned every last drop.

Standing up, he wiped his face. "Warm and sweet," he proclaimed.

"I have to ask...what did that taste like?"

"The finest blend of coffee I've ever tasted."

As he stepped away, a stockholder took his place. "Enough of this shit. Since I hold the most shares in this room, I get to bang her first."

Ethan looked back at the others, who nodded in agreement. Hearing the conversation take place, Ashley wondered, *All of them? Thank goodness I'm not ovulating.*

Her thoughts were interrupted by the re-spreading of her legs. They were bound to the chair again. The deep cloth was yanked from her mouth, making her cough up a storm. She fought her natural gag response.

Ethan's hand touched the blindfold, as the stockholder said, "Leave it. Make her guess, whose cock pleased her...and whose cock just teased her."

From that point on, Ashley was truly in the dark. She heard a belt unbuckle, as a man leaned between her spread legs. A sudden realization overtook her. *I actually prefer to be blindfolded. It's less real, less guilt-ridden when I orgasm. It's almost like I'm safe inside a fantasy.* As fantastical as it was, reality was about to reclaim its place.

The first stockholder took advantage of his early position. Placing his punishing bulbous cock head against her roasted lips, she was suddenly chocked-full of nuts. Without an ability to move, she lay there like a blowup doll.

He unapologetically pounded her, making clear this was no lovemaking session. Ashley was being banged and there was no doubt about it. The man was collecting his benefits, cashing them in all at once.

His 7-inch spear impaled her like a Roman warrior in battle. Squeezing her meaty breasts like a water balloon, they merely burst from the engorged pressure. He leaned in, gnawing the extended nipples.

Swelled with purple, he released her big bags. He yanked a handful of blond hair, testing her pain limits. However, she didn't even feel it. Instead, her senses were hijacked by the primal smacking of her sensitive folds.

Like a prehistoric caveman, the act was for his pleasure only. As little as he cared about foreplay, he cared less about stamina. His loaded cannon fired everything it had. A tsunami of sperm spilled from his slit, overlapping her hole like a tidal wave.

As he withdrew, the pressure inside her declined. Although she couldn't see the next male in line, his difference was surely felt. The 18 year-old worker lowered his pants, carefully guarding his 4-inch ego killer. Being a virgin, he obviously had never taken part in such debauchery. It surely wouldn't last long.

The prior participant's lubricant oozed from the relaxed hole. In one easy slide, the thin, four-inch penis was swallowed by her used box. His glands were glided through the flooded garden, causing him to lose control.

Holding on for his life, he gripped her thighs. The young man grunted, squirting an untapped sperm bank inside her. Streams of fresh frosting continued filling her puffed pastry, as his body trembled more than hers.

In a much different experience than before, his head slowly crashed upon her breasts, sucking her teat. The boy rested upon the motherly vessel. After gently withdrawing, he leaned in for a sloppy, yet sincere kiss. Its truth almost made Ashley cum, though after her morning, it would take much more than that.

Quickly covering his small member, the next man arrived. His wish already granted, the bald VP wanted seconds. As second in charge from the top, his ego demanded more than the others.

Skipping her vagina altogether, he went directly into the forbidden frontier. "No," she said, trying to escape her bonds again.

The VP looked toward his boss, "Boss?"

Ethan nodded in permission. Ignoring Ashley's plea, the VP lowered his pants, revealing a 6-inch cock. Since she knew his voice, his identity was no surprise. Having never liked his arrogance, she wasn't looking forward to being seeded by him. *He's old enough to be my father!* She thought.

Spreading her wider, he wasted no time testing her limits. Already drenched with human lubricant, her soft sphincter prepared for the arrival. Fighting past the tight anal ring, the vice president got his wish. Having grown up in a different time, he'd never dare ask his wife to perform such a deviant act. Mrs. Taylor was *far* from his wife.

Having only tried anal sex under alcohol's influence, Ashley soberly felt every inch. Her lusty cries increased in decibel, threatening to alert the neighbors. Grabbing the nearby tie-gag, Ethan re-stuffed her mouth.

Her moans fought through the gag, begging for mercy. With none in sight, the older man felt like a bull, banging her senseless. The pre-slicked juices allowed him to plunge her with ease. Though, even with the slippery slope, Ashley's anus tightened upon his cock with revenge of its own.

His plan was to hold out, punishing her as long as possible. Though it proved impossible. The VP was the one needing a gag, firing bolts of finely aged wine into her barrel.

The train marched on, as the last was again female. Ethan looked at her, saying, "I guess this one really isn't for you. I'm sure I can think of something else..."

In the midst of his statement, the thin brunette approached her secondhand prize. She removed the gag, allowing Mrs. Taylor's parched mouth to refill. Lifting her shirt, the coworker's tiny A-cups were revealed. Resting the tiny mounds atop Ashley's towering slopes, the brunette beauty kissed the soft mouth with passion. No more mystery remained, as the blindfold was softly slipped off.

Mrs. Taylor was free to see soft palms massage softer thighs. The brunette put the men to shame, treating Mrs. Taylor's treasures with deserved reverence. Word of the girl had spread around the office...she had a hidden streak of dirty deeds. The secret was about to be revealed.

The thinly framed girl dropped to her knees, addressing Ashley's feminine thighs with a long lick. Following a faint trail of saltiness, her strongest senses detected nirvana. For the first time in days, Mrs. Taylor was at ease.

The sea of sperm leaked from deep depths, as the thin coworker dipped a fingernail inside. Swirling a sample upon her finger, she withdrew, taking a taste in her mouth. Her eyes rolled, savoring the smorgasbord of flavors. It was savory, yet sweet.

Using two fingers, the girl wiggled the long appendages into the bed of masculine butter. As the pumping motion began, Ashley bared down. Her stimulated uterus was forced to surrender its stored load, leaking like a sieve. Aimed in an upward movement, thin fingers struck the G-spot, swelling it with sensuality. The men drooled in desire, wishing to acquire an ounce of the magic touch their coworker had.

Having already had some small quakes along her fault-line, Ashley's big bang arrived. A feminine roar sounded from her strained throat, as she writhed so hard, one of her arm restraints came loose. Her eyes opened, seeing the familiar faces she once called friends. Things would never be the same. As reality returned, her hand tried to stop the brunette's progression. Ethan tied it back into place.

A full minute passed, as the spasms continued. The more Ashley came, the more white treasure spilled from her foxhole. One last major spasm shook the table, as two thin knuckles disappeared deeply into Mrs. Taylor's gland.

Circles of dizziness spun around Ashley's head. Just as she began to calm, two feminine fingers were eased into her mouth. They were filled with cum, buttering the bumpy buds of taste.

Making sure Mrs. Taylor got every drop, the brunette went deeply into the throat. Even through the gagging, she made sure every ounce of coworker cum was ingested. Suckling like a feeding fish, she cleaned every ounce.

While Ashley's sucking continued, the brunette kneeled down, burying herself in the offering. Spreading one set of lady lips with another, she curled her tongue in a tight roll. Forming a straw-like shape, she siphoned the remaining white gold.

Licking until every inch was clean, the coworker returned to her feet. Removing her fingers, Ashley's lips were still rimmed with remnants. Like white lip-gloss, the brunette leaned inward to the center of attention.

First, came the lip sucking kiss. The surprise was saved for the second course. A cum-coated tongue worked itself inside Ashley's mouth, depositing the last of her payload.

Although Mrs. Taylor was never a big cum swallower, something changed. Shock filled her brain as she thought to herself, *I crave more.* There was no reason to worry, since there would be many identical opportunities ahead. Not only would she have to repay every cent, the interest would be collected in full.

*****

A thoroughly drained Ashley entered her small space. After her taxing morning, she still had a full day to work, plus overtime. After arriving in her room, she noticed an added calendar on the wall. Her heart hit the ground, as she examined the second X marking the second day.

She shut her eyes, thinking one last thought. *How will I survive an entire year of this? My kids are being raised by marijuana man. I can't go to jail, no matter how much I may want a vacation. No matter how bad it gets.*

As she drifted into a comatose-like sleep, it felt like weeks were spent, safe in slumber. She'd never slept so hard in her life. When Ashley awoke, 6-months had flown by.

In reality, it wasn't actually six straight months of sleep, though it could've been. Each day produced the same results. Whether being banged on office furniture or putting on guest sex shows, it became a job.

There were the days she felt like quitting, going to prison. Then, there were the letters allowed from her kids. She hadn't opened one, knowing it would only make her cry.

Though, as the halfway point arrived, something strange happened. The sexual degradation was starting to lose its intended purpose. The shame became a taboo pleasure in itself. With each new act, Ashley became empowered, instead of weakened.

She finally opened her kids' letter, comforted in the fact they were OK. Sniffing the letter, she was even happier to realize it didn't smell like pot. *Take every positive you can get,* she theorized.

Not only did the tunnel's light begin to shine, she started to see a life after blackmail. *I can't wait to see my kids again, maybe even my husband. Most of all, I can't wait to get back on my feet...so I can return Mr. Cole's depraved hospitality...in full.*

*****

While one-half the equation hurdled the midseason hump, the other grew fearful. *I've only got six months left,* Ethan Cole warned himself. *I've grown accustomed to this, what will I do when it's over?* Though, the thing he truly wondered, *What will I become? Powerless? Control over nothing...nobody?*

He gazed down at his current financial figures, realizing a harsh reality. *Even without her thievery...we're still broke. We're losing customers left and right...forced to raise our prices just to break even. Blaming everything on Ashley made me feel better about my future, bought me time. There's no longer an excuse. In six months, I'll be out of business...broke.*

It was believed that some businesses were fail proof, sex toys being one of them. However, after the government levied a massive sin tax on them, sales nose-dived. The junk food and entertainment industries were also destroyed.

Anger filled his face, as he pulled a bottle of Bailey's Irish Cream from his drawer. Dumping the numbing alcohol into his coffee, he took a sip. Shutting his eyes, he basked in current reality. Looking back down into the glass, the same tired, defeated reflection stared back as before. *How can I stop myself from losing everything?*

The man who forced Ashley into servitude suddenly stared back. Unfortunately for Mrs. Taylor, *that* man was reborn. He reached for a sex toy catalog, featuring the upcoming mega convention. "That's it!" he announced to an empty room. "Why waste time punishing her...when I can profit off of her instead?"

Part Two

CHAPTER FIVE

"But...I'm claustrophobic!" a fearful Ashley Taylor begged her boss, Ethan Cole. A smirk crossed his face, as her vulnerability made him erect.

"You'll live," he said. "If not, you're covered by workers' comp. Your family will be compensated...after I take what I'm owed. Put the nose mask on her, boys."

Three workers approached the curvy, blond bombshell. They were inside Mr. Cole's factory. Every sex toy was manufactured there. Ashley was nude, lying in a square pool of shallow depth.

A small mask was strapped over her nose, pumping air from a thin tube. Her hands were tucked into her sides, cuffed to the walls. Any sharp movement would cost the company money it didn't have.

Mrs. Taylor gasped, seeing a vat of pink slime. *This makes a coffee enema seem like child's play,* she thought. Having once dreaded the workplace gangbangs, she had begun to crave the sexual servitude.

Though back at the 6-month mark, everything changed. The moment Ethan's epiphany was born, the purpose of Ashley's imprisonment was altered. *Why waste time punishing her...when I can profit off of her instead?* Right after that thought, his brainstorming began. The boss explored uncharted waters of perversion, aiming to hook the masses.

He recalled the way Ashley once seduced him. The barflies he brought home nearly knocked her off the Sybian. Though the biggest allure was the office workers. All the men and lone woman couldn't resist her. Like an apple in Eden, he'd use Mrs. Taylor to sell his monumental idea.

His only problem? He hadn't discovered it yet.

The sixth month of captivity went to waste. As Ashley cooked, cleaned, and *entertained*, Ethan all but ignored her. At first, she felt relieved. Though after a while, she began taking offense to it. *Am I not sexy enough to abuse anymore?*

As the seventh month began, Ethan exploded in a fit of fruitless frustration and recklessly kicked-in the bathroom door. The showering beauty gasped, as Mr. Cole tore off the shower curtain. Tossing it on the floor, he dragged Ashley out, sliding her upon it. Lowering his pants, he leapt on top of her. His 8-inch cock aimed for her soapy vagina. With bubbly residue clinging to her lips, he entered with ease.

He pulled her wet hair, wringing it like a blond mop. Pounding her kitty like an agitated pit-bull, an evident anger-bang was on full display. Every muscle in his face tensed and tightened. Ashley was in shock. *Why does he ignore me one minute, force fucking me the next?* She wondered.

She'd find the answer in her boss's eyes. A desperate man stared back, proving it wasn't about *her* crimes anymore. It was something even more personal, eating at his soul. Mrs. Taylor was merely a vehicle to let off steam, a human punching bag.

He pressed her neck down into the wet shower curtain. The water was left on, filling the room with smoky steam. His ramming got so intense she could feel his cock in her upper GI.

With each bang, the two slid further off the slick curtain. At one point, they exited onto cold tile like a child's slip and slide. By the time they neared the door Ethan neared an ejaculation.

The hair pulling got more intense. Ashley's legs flew into the air, as her toenails scraped the travertine surface. Finally, Mr. Cole blasted her full of cum. It was more than he'd ever expelled, dumping warm seed into a steamed cavern.

As he finished, the man collapsed upon Mrs. Taylor's bulging breasts. The grip was released from her hair, taking a few strands with it. His body calmed to a tension-free, stress-relieved stillness. Most importantly, his inspiration was reborn.

"Is there anything else I can do for you, Mr. Cole?" Ashley asked.

He lifted his head in satisfaction. "You've already done it, Mrs. Taylor." Standing up, he stared down at her semen-stuffed oyster. "Go clean yourself."

Her face soured, as she said, "You're the boss."

Mr. Cole's eyes opened wide. *"That's it!"*

"What?"

He pulled up his pants, hurrying from the room. His idea was born, and the plan to profit off Ashley hatched. Sleepless nights of worthlessness were replaced by sleepless nights of purpose.

More months vanished in the re-working of his creation. Beginning the ninth of Ashley's twelve-month sentence, he finally perfected it. Holding up the blue prints, he announced, "Dominated by the Boss!"

On paper, he'd created the closest thing to virtual domination. First, he'd have Ashley's vagina, anus, and mouth immortalized in rubber. Not just outer molds, he'd defy industry standards by emulating her inner tightness, shape, and texture. Electronic sensors would record every thrust and movement of the user's penis.

After that, he'd create a mainframe machine. It was similar to a gyno chair, with a few major differences. At the end of the chair, multiple size and shaped dongs awaited. Attached to mechanical arms, they were to emulate the user. Each fan would get to fuck their most desirous dream, be it a porn star or an unknown seductress.

Another month was put into producing the prototype, to be unveiled at the Mega Sex-Toy Convention. Pouring millions into the product line, it would make or break Ethan's company. Ashley Taylor would grace the cover first; she'd be the first to grace the chair.

After that, the sky was the limit. Porn companies or websites could purchase the mainframe. For a price, they could cast their own stars in the unique rubber. In time, virtual workplaces, principal offices, dungeons, and brothels would be born. They'd be as accessible as a video game. Sensor-based paddles and whips would be created. At $59.99 a pop, fans could take an orifice home at an affordable price.

The last step was producing a mold. The present moment carried heavy weight for Ethan Cole. He stood at the base of Ashley. She was about to be doused with a newly invented liquid rubber.

A plastic fitting was shoved into Ashley's throat. Cringing in fear, she watched a pink waterfall drown her body. Although her hands and ankles were pinned still, she was frozen in fear anyway.

Within moments, the goo swallowed her face, leaving a tiny mask for breath. Her body internally trembled, feeling the liquid begin to solidify.

"Do it now," Ethan ordered two workers.

The men carefully entered the tub, submerging their rubber gloves. One worker steadily aimed for Ashley's honey hole. Heading between her V-shaped thighs, he carefully directed the stiffening sludge into her canal.

Swirling his finger along her velvet folds, the rubber formed perfect shape, texture, and depth. Removing his finger, the hole closed, replicating an exact tightness.

Moving down to her anus, the worker repeated the motion. Pushing hard into her sphincter, the liquid rubber crept through her anal tunnel. The replica slowly stiffened, turning to rubberized gold. As the finger withdrew, the tiny hole retracted, capturing the tantalizing tightness of her savory star.

While one man worked her lower extremities, another focused on the upper. As the breasts took shape, the second worker ran four fingers into her cupped mouth. Although the texture would be carved later, the depth was exact. Her pillowy lips would also be reproduced.

"Get out...before it sets!" Mr. Cole shouted. The men followed instruction, jumping out. "Now we wait," Ethan carelessly announced.

Beneath the pink puddle, Mrs. Taylor fought panic from driving her mad. Though, trapped in complete submission, there was also something hot about it. It didn't hurt that the rubber was forming, filling her with an immense pressure. Fear was being replaced by a warm sting inside her orifices.

The weight of an elephant pushed upon every nerve, hardening into a spongy crust. Her worry turned from panic to orgasmic, knowing she'd have to hold dead still. Within moments, chills crossed her encased body. She broke form, though luckily the mold had set.

Shaking with fire, she came. Stimulated in every hole, the rubber tomb jiggled at the surface, bringing a smile to Ethan's face. To some, it appeared to be an earthquake, though to Mr. Cole, it was the beginning of a windfall.

"Quarter it into sections. Be extra careful removing it from the anus. We can't risk a single tear."

The workers removed long knives, cutting the rubber mass into three sections: the head to shoulders, breasts to vagina, and upper thighs to feet. Each clump was removed carefully, exposing Ashley's unblemished skin.

First the bottom was removed. The middle went next, slowly unearthed from each crack. Finally, the top was lifted, taking the mouth cup with it. Tears streamed Mrs. Taylor's cheeks, as she shook.

Ethan kneeled down to her, removing the nose mask. "You did well, young lady."

His words didn't help, as she continued to cry. "I nearly suffocated!"

"When it's all said and done...it'll be worth it."

"To you!" she shouted.

His smile grew, as he said, "Take a shower, and get some rest. In a few short days...you could be a star."

*****

"Welcome to the Mega Sex Toy Convention!" an announcer's voice shouted from a speaker. It echoed through a massive convention center.

Ten thousand people clogged the crowded booths. Hundreds of companies hocked their latest products, hoping to be the breakout toy of the year. Some hired pricy porn stars to display their contraptions, lending instant name recognition.

There were women in sex swings, swaying in rhythm with their partner's cock. Different paddles and whips were given to customers, allowing them to beat dream girls into submission. Outfits ranged from leather masks to dog collars to furry animals.

Edible sex toys featured 9-inch cock lollypops, fruit rollup thongs, and chocolate vaginas filled with heavy cream.

Needless to say, Ethan's competition was tremendous. If he left the show without a hefty amount of orders, the company was done for. Taking a deep breath, Mr. Cole neared a performance platform.

Multiple stages were set up, allowing companies the limelight. It was a golden chance to shine. Ethan's company got the smallest stage, far from the center. He didn't have the clout of *Adam & Eve* or *Doc Johnson*. Everything hinged upon a novel idea, and one sexual seductress.

Standing next to him, Ashley Taylor wore a black skirt and typical white shirt. It was the cliché office outfit, adding a realistic flair. Even more nervous than her boss, she gazed at the sparse crowd. A few bored men waited around. They didn't know Ashley Taylor from a street hooker, though they only sought hot pussy. Mrs. Taylor certainly fit the mold.

The lack of people increased her self-consciousness. She begged Ethan to use a pseudonym, though he refused. *What if my family sees this? It's broadcast on the web!* She thought.

Her thoughts were quickly distracted by a tall man standing behind her. Ethan nodded at him, he nodded back. He had intense eyes, darkened and slicked hair. The man wore a pricy button-down shirt and slacks, polished shoes. There appeared to be tension between the two men.

Captivated by him, Ashley was interrupted by a less appealing sound. "Are you ready to shine?" Ethan asked.

Returning to reality, an ill look painted her face. "I *think*."

"I don't like that word...or the look on your face," he told her.

"Imagine how I feel."

"That's not my job. Whatever you do...don't get sick. One drop of vomit...I'm ruined."

A wicked look of revenge crossed Ashley's face. *Ruining him sounds good about now.*

"Let me rephrase that," he warned. "You vomit...I'll send you to jail for years of your life. Your contract's not up yet."

She swallowed, forcing the nausea downward. "I won't."

"Since that's cleared up, I expect to see pleasure on your face. You will *orgasm*."

The stressed look increased. "I can fake it."

"Unacceptable! These people buy products for a living...they can spot a fake from 100 miles. You'll cum...and you'll like it."

"Then I guess we'll see how good your product really is."

The announcer's voice sounded on the loud speakers. "Would you please welcome," a pause filled the air, as he gazed at a paper. "Cole Inc.'s very own...*Ashley Taylor*. She'll be displaying their groundbreaking product...*Dominated by the Boss!*"

A tiny smattering of applause followed.

"Go now?" Ashley asked.

"Yeah, now! Remember the script...and say it like you actually mean it!" Ethan pushed her toward the stage.

She stepped upon the platform, stumbling in 3-inch heels. Seeing the three cheering people from the front, further humiliated her. Mr. Cole wasn't even one of them. The announcer shouted, "Another hand for this lovely lady!"

Again, an unflattering smattering of applause filled the air. The buzz belonged to the booths around her, featuring legends of pornography. The announcer stepped up again. "Tell me, who'd like to fuck this scrumptious piece of meat?"

"I'll do it," a few odd-looking men shouted.

"It won't actually be her...but you'll believe it is. This...state of the art vagina, asshole, and mouth...was molded after the real thing."

"Been there...done that," the crowd yelled, booing.

"Not only will you experience *her* authenticity...she'll feel yours. *Real time!*" the announcer shouted.

A few cheers erupted, as the idea seemed to raise a few eyebrows. Some more people walked over, though the crowd was still shamefully small.

A volunteer was brought on stage, led into a privacy booth. Inside, a rubber vagina, ass, and mouth were set up with a viewing screen. It emulated a customer's home experience. The man squeezed inside, shut the door, and yanked his jeans down.

On stage, Ashley sat in the chair, spreading her panty-hosed legs. This time, every person in the small crowd cheered. Her heeled feet were placed into the stirrups, awaiting a circle of plastic dildos. All sensors were linked thru Bluetooth. "Whenever you're ready...stick it in!" the announcer shouted.

"Wait," Ashley said. Everyone got quiet. Taking a deep breath, she got into character. Looking directly into the camera, her voice lowered to a sultry, sexy, smokiness. "What can I do for you today...boss?"

The volunteer spoke into a microphone. "The shirt...rip it open, bitch!"

Another cheer sounded, as she tore the white buttons up the middle. Her thick, braless C-cups spilled out.

"The skirt?" she asked.

"No...rip the pantyhose, show the boss your pussy!" he said in a creepy, low voice.

"Yes, sir," she said, ripping her sheer hose along the vaginal line. Wearing no panties, she revealed a pink slit, identical to her mold. "Are you ready to dominate me...boss?" As the words floated out, the crowd got a collective hard-on.

Instead of verbally answering, the booth-bound man forced his 6 inches inside the pre-gelled mold. His face cringed, feeling the tightness hug him. Suddenly, a simultaneous grunt joined his. Looking upward, his mouth dropped open.

Inside the chair, Ashley was impaled with a 6-inch dildo. Without warning, it plunged its way inside her. She screamed in pained lust, as her voice echoed off the distant convention walls.

Above every sound and sight, it claimed all attention. Having seen many fake demonstrations and stale products, buyers wanted reality. There was no denying it was a real cry from a real woman.

The man in the booth thrust again, pausing. He was shocked at the seamless timing between the two. Testing it a few more times, it was like clockwork. Satisfied with its accuracy, he began pumping like a mating jackrabbit.

Ashley gripped onto the side of the chair, as the hydraulic cock slid in between her ripped pantyhose. Without mercy, the customer drove as deep as possible. With every inch he obtained, the dildo followed.

A steady rhythm formed, along with a larger crowd. She was so caught up in the fucking machine; shock suddenly filled her. Looking at the many faces, her heart pounded with fright. However, it also made her vaginal lair drip with fuel. The exhibitionist in her was unleashed, having never performed for a crowd so large.

They're into me! She silently thought. Her arousal only increased more, as the onlookers grew. With each new tapping of her hole, a new line of crowd members stretched across the arena.

She neared orgasm, as the cock was removed. The crowd cheered, liking the orgasm denial. The volunteer switched to Ashley's fake head, plunging the plastic mouth.

By the time he was inside, the wet dildo flew at her real orifice. With only moments to spare, she opened wide. A vicious gagging was amplified, causing the crowd to roar. She coughed up a sea of saliva, as the plastic cock tapped her throat. Drool spilled from her mouth, as the sensor measured every inch of depth.

At one point, she couldn't breathe. Using his full might, the volunteer clogged the plastic windpipe. Ashley's face turned red, as she tried to pull away. The crowd loved it, watching a stream of spit drench her breasts.

She nearly passed out, as the customer withdrew his cock. A boo filled the air, as the voyeurs wanted her to pass out. Hearing their call for more, the customer went for the ass.

The crowd began to cheer, "Anal! Anal!" Looking upon them, Ashley's face froze in fear. The truth in her eyes was unseen in the porn world. Little did they know, her contract was worth much more than money. Her future freedom was on the line.

*****

Millions of potential consumers stroked their cocks, watching from a live web-feed. As the camera zoomed in on the blonde's assets and girl next-door face, each man leaked with pleasure.

One man in particular, jerked off, while taking a massive hit of potent marijuana. "Oh, that filthy slut is hot! What I'd give to pop that ass! I'll never be so lucky though."

Unbeknownst to him, he'd popped it many times. The man was Ashley's drugged husband, Todd Taylor. His mind had officially turned to mashed potatoes.

*****

Hearing the elation, Ethan Cole nearly wet himself with joy. Ashley looked at her boss, seeing him gaze back at the slick-haired man. The two nodded in approval again.

How do they know each other? Ashley silently wondered. Forced from her thoughts, the dildo was thrust into her tight sphincter. Although her thighs managed to soften the blow, it ripped another hole in the surviving pantyhose. Forced inside her, she squirmed in the chair.

A manly moan sounded from the privacy box, as the volunteer felt Ashley's plastic anal-ring tighten. Her canal choked the plastic invader, virtually bursting his rod.

Her feet pressed against the stirrups. Eventually, Ashley was forced to relax her forbidden flume or risk a perineum tear. Finally settling in place, her focus was recaptured by the crowd.

Mrs. Taylor was shocked to see the entire auditorium fighting for a spot. The anal spectacle was a hit. Rival companies, perspective buyers, and average customers, nearly came to blows, pushing for position.

The cheering began to grow, as they demanded an orgasm. "Cum Ashley! Cum Ashley!"

These people love me! She told herself, suddenly locking eyes with the mysterious man. Mrs. Taylor had never felt such an intense stare. His slicked hair and dark eyes penetrated her deeper than the dildo. Momentarily lost in his burning gaze, Ashley finally broke.

She cried out in pure bliss, feeling pulses of electricity. As her anal canal constricted again, the customer blew a fuse of his own. As he came, the sensors detected it.

Emulating the action, a creamy gel exploded inside her covert cavity. With each pumping, a thicker coating revealed itself. As the booth volunteer withdrew, a sea of white poured from the gaping holes, both real and plastic.

A roar filled the convention. The energy filling the room equaled the Super Bowl, not a sex toy convention. "Toy of the year! Toy of the year!" they shouted, refusing to wait for the vote.

The announcer walked on the stage, bringing Ethan Cole. He handed him the award, holding it up in victory. The crowd rushed the stage, wanting to place orders. Corporations wanted the machine…customers wanted the vagina.

The fans wanted Ashley Taylor.

"Ash-ley! Ash-ley!" they shouted, causing her to blush. Tears rimmed her eyes, as she gazed around, searching for the mysterious man.

He was gone.

CHAPTER SIX

"The orders are coming too damn fast. We can't handle it...need more man power!" the company's Vice President shouted. He ran into Ethan's office with the latest numbers.

Mr. Cole's face matched the panic in the VP's voice. "The bank denied us another loan extension. We're tapped out. I put everything into developing the prototype. In other words...we're broke," Ethan declared.

"So what now? We just fold on the crest of success?"

A look of both dread and hope crossed Ethan's face. He still had a few tricks up his sleeve, though only one would pay off immediately. "Not if I can help it."

After everyone went home for the night, Mr. Cole placed a call. He uncomfortably awaited the results.

A knock sounded on the door, as the mysterious man from the convention entered. The tall, slicked-haired man was named

Thomas, though Ethan called him by another title. "Brother!" Ethan said, rising from his desk to hug him.

As one brother hugged the other, awkwardness filled the room. "What do you want now?" Thomas Cole asked. "I was skeptical at the first invitation...now I'm downright suspicious."

"Can't a man just spend quality time with his brother? Before the sex toy convention, years went by with no contact. We're practically strangers."

Thomas rolled his eyes. "Go sell your bullshit somewhere else. You may have fooled me once, but that's all you're gonna get."

"Such little faith in family."

"Good luck robbing someone else this time," he said, walking out.

"OK, so you were *half*-right. I need your help, though there's something in it for you too. Something you've wanted for a while."

Thomas stopped, turning back around. "What?"

"More company shares."

"I want my original holdings back."

"Don't be foolish. You know I can't do that."

"Why? Because that would make us equals? Partners again? That would be quite the threat to your...egotistical empire."

"Look, you want shares, I want to sell some. We both get what we want."

Thomas paused in thought. "Fifty-one percent. Not a share less."

"You *know* that would leave me with nothing."

"Would serve you right for the shit you pulled."

"Perhaps you'll get revenge someday...just not today. Fifteen percent! That would make you the number two holder. I'll only have 36%."

"Which is all you need to stay on top. Not interested," Thomas said, turning away again.

"I know about your marriage. I know she cleaned you out...took everything."

Thomas stopped in anger. "My divorce is between me and my ex."

"I've been there...let me help you. The dividend checks will yield millions when our new line hits the shelves. It's a sure thing."

"You'll understand if I don't trust your...*sure things*. At least this charade finally makes sense. Inviting me to the convention...was more than brotherly love. I guess I'm not the only one who's broke."

"But you have credit! That's just as good...a loan. You know we're on the edge of glory....you saw *that* crowd yesterday! You saw my girl in action!"

"Ashley Taylor," Thomas said, suddenly coming to life.

Noticing the expression, Ethan found his brother's weakness. "You like what you saw?"

Thomas quickly calmed himself. "Who didn't? She created a buzz...people would kill for."

"My point exactly! Join me in fulfilling her potential! Get *that* loan. Think about it...the Cole brothers...reunited. We'll take this company where *we* always imagined."

"Where *I* always imagined. You stole my dream."

"No, sir...I legally collected it. Collateral is just a casualty of business."

"Funny, I call it cashing in on misfortune."

"Either way, they spell the same word. *Profit*. I'm asking you to reinvest in your dream. Let's mend the past...by taking the future of porn by storm. All I need is the capital to do it!"

Thomas paused in heavy thought. "How much will it cost?"

"About...40...50...thousand.

"What do you think I'm made of? Hell, why not take out $100,000 while I'm at it?" Thomas mocked.

"Now that you mention it, I was going to ask...if you could do such a thing. Just in case...I need a tiny bit more. Just a back up plan."

"Yeah, I know you and your back up plans."

"When the millions roll in...I'll pay it back myself!" Ethan ensured.

"I think you mean...*if* the millions roll in."

"When. You said it yourself...Ashley's a sure thing."

"If I'm gonna do this again...I wanna be a part of the process, marketing, advertising...talent."

"All of it. Brother, you'll be by my side for the first strike. It's a web ad...Internet spot. You can meet Mrs. Taylor in person...watch the action live!"

"Action...as in sex?" he questioned.

"You'll see things you never imagined possible. So we have a deal?"

Thomas inhaled deeply, dreading to shake the devil's hand. Though to start a fire, he'd have to get close enough to make a spark. Thomas Cole shook on it. "Deal."

*****

"My face is really on a box!" Ashley said in disbelief. "Along with my vagina, butt-hole, breasts...oh shit!" Her embarrassment increased with each realization. Holding the encased product in front of her, she didn't know what to think. On one hand, she was star struck with thoughts of national exposure. On the other, the *bodily* exposure shamed her deeply. There was something about print that made it more real, permanent.

"Fear not...the world's already seen it. Besides, it's merely a launch pad to stardom," Ethan Cole said, standing in a studio soundstage. Minus the gyno chair, the room was a replica of Ethan's office. Everything from the oak desk to a square-frame coatrack was present. Each drawer was stocked to perfection, overflowing with office supplies. As excessive and unnecessary as it seemed, everything had a purpose.

Ashley's plastic vagina console was set up, as two digital cameras made a practice run. They were tasked with capturing every naughty moment, planned or not. Although not broadcast live, it would be downloadable on the company's website. Mrs. Taylor didn't grasp the reality of it yet, though by day's end, her career path would veer sharply left.

A tattooed, muscular man with a shaved head approached. His suit and tie didn't defuse his toughness or familiar face. *I've seen this man somewhere before,* Ashley thought to herself.

Ethan approached, "I'd like you to meet Mr. Jake...*The Snake*...Johnson. In case you didn't know...the man's a porn legend."

It suddenly hit her, as she remembered her husband's smut viewing sessions. She recalled another odd detail. *Wasn't he doing bondage in that film? Why would he be here?* She also remembered being in awe of his massive cock. "You're the guy...with the really big penis," she said, blushing in embarrassment.

"Hence the name...*snake*. Twelve inches to be exact," he bragged.

"You're in this *commercial* too?" she asked.

"I am," he said with a deceptive smile upon his face.

"Which reminds me, time is money," Ethan shouted. "Places people."

Ashley straightened her work outfit, donning the typical black and white uniform. Her pantyhose were pre-ripped at the crotch. She sat in the gyno chair, placing her feet in the stirrups. After a few mindless words, she'd be impaled with the dildos.

Her partner had a private conversation with Ethan Cole. *What could they be talking about?* She wondered. Her thoughts were suddenly interrupted by a mysterious face gazing from behind them.

He was not part of the discussion, banished off to the side. It was Thomas Cole. *The man from the convention. Who is he? What's he doing here?* Their gazes met again, as Ashley lost herself in the same way. She wasn't even naked, yet he still looked at her with such intensity, admiration. *There's just something comforting in his eyes.*

"Let's do it!" Jake *The Snake* shouted.

"Camera's ready," Ethan directed. "Quiet on the set!"

The red light was activated, as Ashley took a deep breath.

"Action!" Cole yelled.

An offstage announcer spoke into a microphone. "Jake *The Snake* Johnson's accountant has been a bad girl. He can't dominate her in real life...but needs to let off some steam. Is there a way?"

"Only in my fantasies," he shouted.

"Wrong!" the announcer proclaimed.

"You mean...there is?" he asked in an over-the-top way.

"*Dominated by the Boss!*" the announcer's voice was deepened and affected with reverb. "Simply stick your cock inside Ashley Taylor's vagina, and let the domination begin."

He removed his clothes, revealing a ripped body. A 12-inch python spilled out, swaying as he approached the plastic vagina. He placed his bulbous head at the dripping plastic entrance. Slipping inside, his face contorted with pleasure. Although it was written in the script, the surprised reaction was real. "Damn, that's some good pussy!"

Right as he sank inward, the 12-inch dildo was thrust into Ashley. She cried out in immediate shock. Pre-lubed, it did nothing to prepare her for the massive invader. He pumped away, feeling the plastic tighten in sync with the real flesh.

"She's like a virgin," he said, throwing in an unscripted line. Ethan liked it.

As the rod sank deeper, Ashley turned her head toward Thomas Cole. The lust in his eyes turned the painful pounding into pure pleasure.

As Jake's 12-inch cock filled the expanding canal, his plastic part matched it. Veins swelled from his neck, as the professional sexpert couldn't believe how quickly he was going to cum. The man had gone for hours in his movies.

Ashley neared an eruption as well. Hers wasn't triggered by the machine, it was aroused by the bulging pants of Thomas Cole. He untucked his shirt, trying to mask embarrassment, though it only brought more attention.

Within moments, Jake *The Snake* stiffened, blasting a thick load inside her rubber cavern. Ashley broke too, feeling the massive plastic reach new depths. She gripped the chair's edge, grinding her feet on the stirrups. Her thighs tightened upon the phallus, feeling the fake load spray her.

Jake withdrew, causing the dildo to follow. Ethan instructed a cameraman to zoom on the escaping ejaculate. Then, he instructed the other camera to get a close up of Ashley's face.

After catching her breath, Mrs. Taylor remembered her last line. The spent woman looked in the camera, saying, "I've been *Dominated by the Boss*."

"Cut!" Ethan yelled.

"Can I go clean up?" Ashley asked.

"Stay there...one more take," Ethan shouted, pointing at a stagehand. The worker pulled the mobile, square coatrack forward.

"Again?" Ashley asked, paying no attention to the new prop. "That wasn't good enough?"

"It was great...though this time, I'd like to try something different," Ethan said deviantly. Looking over at Jake, he smiled. "You're good for another round?"

"I'm just getting warmed up," he said, ready to try the real thing.

"Action!" Ethan shouted.

The announcer repeated the script. "Jake *the snake* Johnson's accountant has been a bad girl. He can't dominate her in real life...but needs to let off some steam. Is there a way?"

"Yeah...though not with this plastic bullshit," Jake said, adding the bullshit line to Ethan's displeasure. Everything else was as scripted.

Ashley's face cringed in confusion. She looked over at Mr. Cole, who refrained from eye contact. Then she gazed at Thomas, who seemed angry. He was not consulted on any changes.

Jake headed towards the desk drawers, emptying them. Gathering all the office supplies, it was time to grant them life. He grabbed a roll of black duct tape. Next, he walked over to Ashley, lifting her into his arms. Fear painted her eyes.

"What are you doing?" she whispered.

"Dominating my worker," he said, carrying her over to the square rack. Placing her at the wooden beam, he pulled her arms upward. Peeling the thick masking tape, he wrapped both her wrists to the structure.

Arriving at her ankle, she began to kick. The strong porn star laughed, catching her appendage in flight. He taped her ankle to the coatrack beam. By the time he got to the other one, she had given up. Ashley was secured in an X-shaped pattern.

The nervous woman looked over at Mr. Cole, seeing the approval on his face. It was clearly part of his plan. She was about to graduate from cover girl to porn star. Needing a way to make more money, nothing would do it like a hot bondage film.

The final cherry was placed on her face. Jake taped her lips and eyes shut, leaving her mute and blind in his control.

Tossing the tape aside, he grabbed sharp scissors, cutting her buttoned shirt up the middle. Her bulbous breasts spilled out. Next, her skirt was cut from the bottom up, falling to the floor. Left in only sheer pantyhose, they were cut up the crotch, slicing a bigger slit than before. It traveled from her clitoris to ass crack. Otherwise, the fabric remained on her body.

Done with the scissors, he reached for the next workplace tool. Grabbing a mixture of paperclips and rubber bands, he returned to his blinded victim. The dominant male stretched the tiny bands, forcing them around Ashley's C-cup breasts.

After letting go, they swelled a half-cup size. She jolted, shocked by the instant pressure. Puffed into a massive ball, the breasts turned a slight shade of purple. It forced her nipples to reach gargantuan lengths, only seen on the pages of National Geographic. The cameras sucked up every inch.

Bending the paper clips, he rigged them to just fit her nipples. The pinched metal clamped her aureoles. She muffled, squirming from the stinging sensation. The red darts swelled with swollen pleasure. She quieted her own body. *Does it hurt or feel good? Is it possible for nipples to explode?*

While Mrs. Taylor pondered her fate, Jake *The Snake* moved on. He returned with a yardstick ruler. *Snap!* The long, thin wood swayed against the curvy blond's skin. She moaned through the tape, pulling at her restraints. A perfect red line crossed her bubbly bottom. *Crackle!* He whipped her again. All he needed was a *Pop*, and she'd be a bowl of *Rice Krispies.*

He followed by rubbing her cheeks. Ethan pointed at a cameraman, realizing he was only getting one angle. "Get *that* footage!" he frantically whispered.

The cameraman rushed to capture the back angle. He zoomed in, staying far from the other camera's gaze. Kneeling down, Jake caressed the smooth skin with his hand. He blew on the natural red heat with his lips. The combined sensations soothed and tickled. As he felt chills rise upon her flesh, he stood up again.

Caressed into a false sense of security, Ashley was spanked again. The strength was even harder than the prior two. However, the combined pleasure and pain stimulated her more.

After each new spanking, she was relieved with another caressing touch. Her brain was clogged with confusion, unsure whether to activate its sensors of fear or acceptance.

Having comforted her stinging red behind, he prepared for one last blow. Saving the hardest for last, he unleashed his power. As the spanking landed, the thin wood snapped in two.

Pushed to a new level, Ashley shook with orgasm. Her pores extended so far, they nearly exploded. The squeezed breasts, pinched nipples, gently caressed curves, and hard whipping pushed her beyond humanity. Her body continued to quiver, hung like processed meat.

Grabbing a thick marker, Jake re-engaged her. Uncapping the writing utensil, the smell of sweet ink filled the air. Placing the cool tip at her upper back, she bucked again. Holding her still with his large hands, he wrote, *cock-whore*.

The hind cameraman zoomed in on the writing.

Next, the male porn star wrote, *Use my pussy and ass.* He followed those words with a downward arrow, pointing to the edge of her crack. Recapping the marker's tip, he leaned upon his knees. Spreading her hole, he rimmed her savory star with his slick tongue.

Afterward, he placed the tip of the round marker at her sphincter. Twirling it, he slowly drilled into her tense cavity. He wrapped his hand around her waist, pushing on her stomach, watching the invader enter her anus.

She muffled again, as her body stiffened. Feeling it enter the anal ring, she yanked at the tight tape. Her actions only made the intensity grow. The marker continued into her dark cavern, nearly disappearing.

Ashley's body remained in an atrophied state. Jake rose to his feet. His 12-inch cock stood at full attention. It was as red and swollen as his captive's ass cheeks. He traced his hands down her curvy hips. Feeling his touch, she managed to relax a bit.

"You're mine," he whispered into her ear, rubbing his hard staff upon her warm ass. A trail of pre-cum leaked in his wake, creating a human ointment. His bulbous head snuck down her cheek-line.

He slid his man-meat along her slicked folds. Drops of Ashley's love fluid smeared his glands, as he pushed into her primed vagina. Jake's cock put the plastic impostor to shame. Sliding deeper inside her creamy canal, he was doused with a warm welcome. Mrs. Taylor felt her innards stuffed the max, as the inhuman cock permanently reshaped her. She'd be forever ruined for anyone of smaller size.

Seventy-five percent in, he bottomed out, hitting her cervix. Refusing to be limited, he pushed harder. Ashley's body trembled. Her vagina was forced to new dimensions, expanding like California during the gold rush.

With each thrust, Jake's cock sank deeper inside. Grabbing his captive's wide hips, he wouldn't ease until reaching his veiny base. He knew he'd arrived when Ashley moaned so loud she'd separated the sticky tape from her lips.

Hearing it, Jake reached over, covering her mouth with his hand. Fully inside her, he let the pumping begin. Frantic puffs of air sailed from Ashley's nostrils, cooling her master's hand.

Officially adapted to his size, Mrs. Taylor's vagina fully accepted him. With each thrust, her G-spot was pleasurably assaulted. His cock-head tapped her uterine wall, making it feel like he was in her stomach.

All of Ashley's pleasure centers were activated. Her nipples tingled with fire, anus tensed with tremors, and vaginal canal ached in wet lust. She neared another orgasm, as Jake beat her to it.

Withdrawing from her in porn-style, he shot his seed into her crack. Marshmallow cream coated her holes, slowly spilling like a river of liquid snow.

Feeling the slick slide, Ashley's thighs tightened. No longer stuffed with Jake's cock, her gaping-hole still felt its phantom presence. Squeezed with her inner strength, she shuttered in mind-blowing orgasm. Her taped eyes shuttered in fits, rolling into her brain. At one point, she convulsed so hard, the marker was ejected from her anus.

Backing up, Jake watched in amazement. He was captivated by her authenticity. In a business full of fakers, he'd never seen such truth displayed on the screen. *This girl can go a long way,* he told himself.

Continuing to spasm, Ashley remained taped to the pole. "Keep recording!" Ethan told his cameramen, wanting to capture every last jolt.

Thomas Cole approached him. "End it already! She's hanging there like a corpse. Any pleasure's been spent. At least give her an *ounce* of dignity."

"Back off," he warned.

"You told me I'd have a say."

"You do...but I supersede it. She stays there until I say so."

"I knew it. The good brother bullshit ends quicker than it began. You get my money, and the scumbag returns."

"You'll get paid...that's what matters."

"No...that's what matters to *you*. I was hoping to help run a company...like the one I created. You remember that day...don't you...*Mr. Cole?*"

Ethan ignored the accusation. "Maybe you'll have your chance...when I'm dead," he said in a snotty manner. "Until then, just collect your dividends and let the businessmen handle it."

Thomas took one last look at Ashley's hanging, limp body. *Ethan didn't even let me meet her. The bastard couldn't even keep that promise. I was hoping it wouldn't come to this, but he pushed me to it. If he can't stick to the deal, I'll find a way to stick the deal to him.*

CHAPTER SEVEN

Ashley Taylor hung from a studio ceiling by chains, bound at the wrists. Suspended in the air, her arms were pulled to the straining point. A vibrator was stuffed in her, held by her tensed thighs. Her nipples were covered in hardened candle wax. Being her tenth film in five days, there wasn't much that shocked her anymore.

A masked man spanked her with an eager hand. She shuddered with lust, swaying through the air. The camera lens was directly in front of her, shining a reflection back. *I'm like a piece of meat,* she told herself. However, it was no longer a point of shame. As she shuddered in punishing orgasm, something occurred to the once uptight woman. Not only did she accept her new role, she embraced it. *I'm Ashley Taylor, porn star.*

After the shoot, she cleaned her vagina with wet wipes. Ethan joined her. "I want to be paid for my work," she said in bitterness.

"You're already paid, Mrs. Taylor...by not going to jail. After the contract's up, we'll discuss finances."

"How do you know I'll stick around?"

He leaned in, "Because *you* know...like *I've* always known. Ashley Taylor is a natural born slut."

She was both offended and oddly turned on by the statement. "Well, cash in on this *slut* while you can...my freedom's closer with each day."

"Just in case you'd like to know, the internet went crazy for your films. We sold as many downloads in one day...as we sold vaginal units. You were the top trend on three major search engines and twitter. Do you know what that means?"

"Someday soon, you'll be rich. I'll still be your poor slave."

"Correct."

She finished cleaning herself, throwing the wet wipe in a trashcan. "Greedy bastard."

"I'll take that," he said, retrieving it from the garbage.

"What could you possibly do with it?"

"Auction it. Just remember Mrs. Taylor, greed is not a crime...unlike embezzlement."

"What's next? Auctioning me off?"

A look of exploitation filled his eyes.

Ashley's mouth hung open. "You wouldn't!"

*****

Thomas Cole entered a bar, sitting upon a stool. He slumped, staring down into the dull surface. It matched his tired face. The man had been used by everyone dear to him. First it was his brother, screwing him out of his own business. Then his wife left him for another man, taking his kids and money.

Finally, Ethan returned to drive the final nail. After spending half his loan on the shares, Thomas had $60,000 left. He planned to just pay it back, having nothing else to invest in.

"What can I get ya?" the bartender asked.

"Something to numb pain."

The older gentleman thought long and hard. He reached behind the bar, placing an icepick upon the surface. "Good enough?"

He cringed, hit with a dose of reality. Deciding against the lethal weapon, he changed his mind. "Something a little less lethal. At least, for now."

Removing the ice pick, the bartender grabbed a glass. Placing it on the desk, he filled it with straight vodka. "Never been a fan of Russians...though they did something right. Cheers."

"I've got nothing to cheer, friend," Thomas said, sucking the alcohol down in one shot.

As Thomas's face soured, the bar tender placed the bottle next to him. "Some extra medicine...on the house," he said.

"Thanks." Thomas pushed away the glass, taking a swig.

A buzz began to form next to him. A few men pulled out their Internet phones, while others gathered around the adjacent man.

"I'd pay anything to bang *that* broad," the bar patron yelled.

Having once made a similar statement about Ashley, Thomas leaned to the side. "Bang who?"

"*That* porn star...Taylor or something. Hot blond. Her people are auctioning a night of porn star screwing for the highest bidder tonight. It's about to begin."

Shock filled Thomas's face, as he thought, *Is there any level my brother won't stoop to?* "Are you bidding?"

"Yeah right. You got 50-G to loan me? At *least* that much. That's what they're sayin' anyway."

An idea struck Thomas. *The loan could get me an audience with her...in private. Forget sex...I seek revenge.* With nothing else to lose, he pulled out his phone, activating the internet.

On the screen, his brother's image shined back. A nude and embarrassed Ashley joined his side. "This once in a lifetime opportunity awaits you. Ordinary Joes...like yourselves...have a shot to use this woman in every way. Short of snuffing her, of course. That costs extra," he laughed obnoxiously, as Ashley's face tightened in anger.

Thomas focused on Mrs. Taylor, seeing the bitterness on her face. He was willing to bet his future on shared dislike. No one could crush Ethan like Ashley, since she held the key to his success.

Ethan stepped up. "For one lucky man or woman...your fantasy is about to come true. Ready your checkbooks, and place your digital bids."

The younger Cole gazed down at the bid button. Without hesitation, he pressed it. A timer counted down from 5 minutes. *Let it ride,* he told himself. Thomas typed in every last scent to his name. *$60,000.*

"Son-of-a-bitch...we got a real player here! Sixty big ones!" the customer next to Thomas yelled, igniting a cheer from the rowdy group. They rushed over, crowding around him. They examined the screen. "She's worth every penny!"

An empowered Cole placed his bid. Another cheer erupted, as his screen returned to Ashley and Ethan. Focused on Mrs. Taylor's face, Thomas said, "She's worth more than money."

A buzzer sounded as the five-minute mark expired. The crowd hung over his shoulder, anxiously awaiting the announcement. An envelope was brought to Ethan Cole, who eagerly opened it up.

Pulling out the paper, he gazed at it. His eyes opened wide, as the blood drained from his face. Ethan's breath matched his heart's pace. Beads of sweat poured from his head. Wiping it off, he suddenly realized the empty silence. There was no other choice but to announce. "We have a winner," he said in an agitated tone.

Ashley watched in confusion. *He was so upbeat a moment ago, what changed?*

"Congratulations...Mr. Thomas...*Cole.*

Mrs. Taylor's confusion increased. *What an odd coincidence...the same last name? No,* she thought. It *couldn't be relation.* She brushed the thought off.

"I did it!" Thomas shouted, as the bar patrons exploded in cheer. "A round on me!" The cheering continued as he suddenly realized, *Shit, I'm broke.*

*****

Thomas took a nervous breath, approaching a ritzy hotel suite. Before he could enter, he was intercepted by Ethan.

"I tried calling you for days," Ethan said angrily.

"I was busy...preparing for my prize."

"Where'd you get that kind of money? The dividends aren't even close to paying out yet. The shares haven't even begun their climb."

"Someone suggested I get a bigger loan than necessary. I'd say it was wise advice."

A look of regret filled Ethan's face. "Don't mention a word about our relations or business deals. Nothing. Remember, I can make sure any future profit checks...get lost for while."

"What do you have to fear? Do you think she'll respect you less...when I tell her you're a snake? Trust me...*she* knows more than anyone by now. If you'll excuse me...I have a date with a star."

He entered the room, shutting the door behind him. Ethan Cole gulped, feeling a loss of control he hadn't felt in a while.

*****

Thomas entered a posh room, immediately struck by a stimulating sight. Crimson rose pedals covered silk sheets, tracing Ashley's curved body. Her smooth skin shined in candlelight, contrasting a black nighty. Breasts heaved from a low cut cleavage-line, lips peeked from a short bottom. Black, thigh-high stockings rose to the edge of her soft thighs, stopping before her panty-less poon.

A silent gasp sounded from Ashley, though it wasn't a displeased one. Although the two had never shared words, their gazes were familiar, like old souls. *The man from the convention. He was also at the camera shoot. Why is he following me? Who is he?* However, she quickly forced the thoughts from her mind, remembering her job. She was tasked with making him feel like $60,000.

The younger Cole was rendered speechless. "Umm...I'm...Thomas."

Mrs. Taylor sat up slowly, opening her legs in a teasing manner. Her soft feet touched the ground. She rose, approaching the winning bidder. "Hi, Thomas. As you know, I'm Ashley. Tonight, I'll make all your fantasies come true."

She held his hand, walking him toward the bathroom. Upon entering, a large marble tub was filled with rose pedals. Ashley placed his hands upon her soft skin, sliding them up her black nighty. Although Thomas didn't intend to have sex with her, his plans were evolving with every touch. Every inch of her pale skin melted beneath his fingers.

The higher his hands traveled, the more her pores extended. His journey was slow, caressing every inch. He eventually reached her mystic pearls, grasping the bulbous breasts.

Their eyes connected, as Thomas massaged her throbbing mammaries. Her nipples pushed at his palms, making him push back. Her red tips were so erect, they managed to lift his hands.

She returned the favor, sneaking her hands into his shirt. Her long nails slid up his six-pack stomach, tickling his chest.

Continuing upward, she lifted his shirt off. His hands were removed from her nighty, making the task possible. As his neck presented a tempting target, she sucked on it, adding nibbles and shapely red kisses.

Thomas's eyes rolled at the feeling. He'd wanted to stop her, though couldn't bring himself to. After covering every inch of his neck, she traveled downward to his chest. Working her way through a neat dusting of hair, she rimmed his nipple. Running her tongue in circles, the tiny nub rose.

He squirmed, as she gently bit down, tugging with her teeth. Freeing him from the sensitive shock, she followed his trail of paradise. Reaching his waistline, she began to unbutton his pants.

Reality suddenly came back to the man. "Wait!" He forced himself to stop her. "You need to know something...it could change your mind."

"What?"

"I'm Thomas Cole. Ethan's brother."

Having heard the name mentioned, she'd never believed it possible. A look of shock filled her face. "But...you're handsome...nice...*human*! Are you sure you weren't adopted?"

"No. Look, to my knowledge...I'm not your number one fan. I didn't bid to win some contest...or even sex for *that* matter. No offense."

"You tell a girl you don't want her...it's pretty offensive."

"No, please...I'm not saying I don't want sex with *you*. Listen, when I first saw you at the sex toy convention...I was floored."

"Oh really? I didn't even notice you were there," she falsely said in hurt pride.

"Well, I noticed you. I thought you were the most beautiful woman on the earth."

"Getting a little bit better...keep going."

"It's not a pickup line. There's an allure about you...men would kill for. I'd have killed for it, if there weren't something greater to discuss. Something that's haunted me for years."

"What?"

"My brother."

"How does this relate to that?"

"No. I did it to destroy him. You see, more than family...he's my enemy."

Mrs. Taylor dropped upon her knees. "Then I believe that makes us allies. Let's discuss the details afterward," she said, continuing to unbutton his pants.

He couldn't believe it, feeling them drop to his ankles. Thomas's cock matched his brother's 8-inches, though his was thicker. It certainly was more appetizing to Ashley. Her mouth widened, aligning with the mushroom head.

Resting upon the warmed tile, she led his oozing obelisk into her wanting mouth. She gripped the base with her hand, forcing it to swell even more. Veins bulged as his spear turned a faint shade of maroon.

He gasped, lost in her touch. Although his wife recently left him, they were done long before that. Ever since he'd lost his business, his confidence eroded. As his monetary worth sank, so did his husbandly value. She remained with him, though sought *companionship* elsewhere.

Ashley expertly slid Ethan's cock along her tongue. His glands were soaked in saliva as she slowly devoured it. He moaned, feeling his head worked into her esophagus.

She reached around, gripping hold of his muscular ass cheeks. They tightened, as she used them to propel her into his pole. Thomas's body began to tremble, forced to impale the blond bombshell by her own hands.

Her tongue detected the rising spunk, causing her to withdraw. Mrs. Taylor was determined to provide the money's worth. Taking him by the hand, she led Thomas to the steaming bath.

The sweet scent of sizzling rose pedals filled the air, boiled from the water. Ashley began to lift her nighty, as Thomas finally took charge. Running his hands up her curved ass cheeks, he traced her hourglass figure.

Black silk was pinched between his fingers, slid above her bouncing breasts. Hard nipples peeked out, revealing her teardrop treasures. Her hands reached for the air, inviting total nudity.

Fully disrobed, Mrs. Taylor grabbed Thomas's hand again, stepping into the round tub. The water danced upon her entrance, commanded by the squatting beauty. Her eyes closed, absorbing heat into her skin. Vapors rose, softening her shapely image with an angelic glow. Opening her eyes, she didn't speak a word. Her come-hither stare spoke volumes.

Thomas's rod stiffened more. He stepped into the tub, immediately sinking. Leaning back, he claimed the bottom position for himself. His face cringed, feeling the heat sting his sensitive cock. Ashley climbed on top, soothing the burn with her human aloe.

As Mrs. Taylor's vaginal lips snuffed the manly torch, she sank to his cock's base. The rose flavored water seeped inside her, puffing her inner cavern to new extremes. She wrapped her arms around Thomas's head, legs around his waist, and leaned into him.

Methodically pumping, her nipples bobbed in and out of the water. The altering sensations of hot and cold added to her stimulation. Pressing against his chest, her breasts were pleasurably squashed, skin upon skin.

Gravity naturally propelled her into his lips. She fought it, instructed not to kiss a fan. However, she couldn't deny the apple, which had long tempted her from afar. With all the sex she'd had, it felt different than the others. Of course, they used her; he held her.

Their noses touched, creating one joint breath. He inhaled her cherry scented shampoo, while she breathed his spicy cologne. Ashley prepared to engulf his lips, though Thomas beat her to it. As their lips engaged, their tongues slow danced a romantic waltz.

Passion seeped from them as Mrs. Taylor's speed increased. Her thighs began milking his thickness, creating more frictional fire. Waves filled the tub, creating a whirlpool of red petals. The faster she rode him, the more her nipples chaffed his strong chest.

Her arms nearly strangled his neck, as her canal choked his cock. With each landing, warm water slapped her swollen clit. Suddenly, Thomas returned her embrace, squeezing her even tighter.

A deep grunt filled the air, flavoring her watery vagina with pent up seed.

Feeling an added heaviness swim through her, Ashley followed suit. Shivering in hot chills, her canal clamped down upon his cock. A blast of water bubbled out of her heaving box. Some of Thomas's sperm floated to the top.

The two continued to convulse, as Ashley crashed upon him. Burying her face into his neck, she felt vulnerable. Her orgasm was more than physical...it was emotional. In reality, it was the first one in a long while. Her quick breaths gave him goose bumps, making him jitter. Ashley redirected her head on his shoulder.

"Was it worth $60,000?" she asked him.

"No," he said to her surprise. "There's no price you could put on that."

A smile painted her face. "Thank you. It's been a long time since someone's complemented me. At least without using harsh words like *pussy*."

"Ethan was never the complementary type."

"Before Ethan."

"You mean...your husband?"

She nodded. "He's...high. Ok, more like officially a drug addicted vegetable. What can one expect?"

"I understand. Either way, he's a lucky man."

She blushed again at the sincerity of the compliments. "Can I ask you something personal?"

"We're sitting here naked, how much more personal can it get?" Thomas asked.

"True. What happened between you and your brother? The rift seems irreparable."

"It is. You see, this company was once mine."

"You owned it?"

"I did...at least in conception. He agreed to invest with me...fifty-fifty partnership."

"What happened?"

"Against my best wishes, he convinced me to expand quicker than we were ready to. He kept pushing me, more stores, more products, even though he knew the clientele just wasn't there. The Internet was still in a growth phase, and customers weren't...out of the sex toy closet."

"Didn't he fail too? He was half the company."

"He would've...had he not used me as the guinea pig. He always was a business savvy guy, I was the dreamer. He exploited *that* weakness when we were kids...just like he did back then."

"How'd he do it?"

"I was tapped out for loans...therefore, I borrowed my half from him. I signed everything over, assuring him full control. I had to get a real job, pay the bills. Do you believe that bastard promised he'd never leave me broke. Yet, he suddenly was too busy to take my calls."

"That guy really *is* a snake!"

"Yeah. There isn't a day that goes by...I didn't imagine what this company could've been. My luck...he'll ruin himself before I get the chance."

"How so?"

"By hanging himself with the same rope...growing too fast, borrowing too much."

"Why not play his game...switch roles? Buy him out once the ship goes down."

"He'd never agree to sell to me, too much pride."

Ashley paused in thought. "Not to you...but what about me?"

"To no one. Not unless he thought it benefited him."

Ashley thought deeply. "How much stock does he own?"

"After selling to me...about 40%. The rest is distributed to other shareholders."

"Oh yeah...I met a few of them. Will they sell me their shares?"

"For a fortune. These aren't men of principle, and they certainly don't give a damn about our spats."

"I don't have a fortune, but I do have another incentive."

"What could you give them...they don't already have?"

She stood up, revealing her dripping, nude body. "This."

"You'll fuck them...*all*?"

"Let's just say...I'll do anything it takes."

"You'd do that for me?"

"I'll do it for us. You make the offer...I'll deliver the goods."

CHAPTER EIGHT

Ashley trembled, waiting in a large lobby. The building was another ritzy hotel, even pricier than the last. However, there was no suite reserved for sex. A spacious conference room awaited the sexy starlet, and the company stockholders awaited the curvaceous blond. Thomas Cole contacted each man, requesting a private shareholder meeting. It was free from Ethan's presence or knowledge.

Thomas exited the room, joining Mrs. Taylor in the lobby.

"What took you so long?" she asked.

"Asking a bunch of millionaires to temporarily sell their shares for a dollar...takes *a little* convincing."

"Well? Will they?"

"They said no."

She stood up, "Of course, they did. At least we tried."

"Until...I told them your offer."

Silence covered her face. "Which one?"

"The human buffet."

"Gang bang?"

"Yeah."

"When?"

"Now."

She inhaled deeply, exhaling slowly. "How many?"

"Not including myself...there are ten."

"You're not joining?"

"No. After having you for myself...it would only be a let down."

She smiled at the compliment, quickly returning to her worries. "Will I have to sign anything?"

"Yeah. The deal is...you get 6 to 8 months to work your magic. In that time, you'll have to force Ethan to sell. The shares should take a short dip due to Wall Street's lack of confidence. They don't like newbies or chaos. If he thinks the ship's sinking, he'll grab the last life vest."

"Convincing me it'd be better to stay on the ship. The better deal."

"You got it. If you don't work your butt off...he may be right. You'll have to prove you can turn profit. Anyway, at that point...you'll resell our shares back at a dollar. You'll still be the majority holder, owner. How does that sound?"

"Confusing."

"Imagine trying to sell them on that."

"You must have a way with words."

"There were only two words that made it happen. *Ashley Taylor.*"

"Why?"

"You still don't see it, Ashley. This company is already yours. It's nothing without its star...its face. Those men aren't fools, they realize the sudden notoriety was *yours*. In all of Ethan's years, he never got us off the shore. But your...natural sex appeal...has given us a chance. *They* believe in you...*I* believe in you."

Thomas spoke with such passion in his voice, Ashley's nerves melted away. She stood up, possessing a newfound conviction and confidence. "It's time to make good on a deal."

"Are you sure you're ready for this?"

"I was born ready. I'm Ashley Taylor, porn star."

*****

The conference room door flung open. Ten horny men in suits encircled a glossy conference table. Thomas followed her in, closing and locking the door behind him.

Every eye fixated upon the hourglass-shaped beauty, strutting by. Her sequined black dress sparkled in the room light, shining as brightly as her black heels. As she made her way to the room's front, her curved hips swayed like a stalking lioness. Ashley Taylor had attitude.

Facing the men, light illuminated her green eyes. Ashley captivated the room with her ultra blond hair, professional make up, and natural sexuality. She commanded celebrity attention. A few of the men recognized her from Ethan's conference room. Though they looked at her like a new woman, feeling small in her larger-than-life persona.

Thomas handed her the freshly drawn contract, having her sign it. Unlike his brother, she knew he was worthy of her trust. Then he pointed at the table. "After you, Mrs. Taylor."

Library-like silence filled the air. Ashley kicked her heels off, left in black thigh-high hose. She leapt upon the table's surface, walking down the line. With each step, she kicked their papers and personal items off. The shocked men quickly cleared everything before she smashed it. With each step, they saw a tiny thong-line peek from her crack.

She returned to the middle. "Well boys. Come dominate me."

One more tense moment of silence reigned, as a rush of testosterone filled the air. Rising from their seats, each man kicked off his shoes, yanked off his tie, and tossed their clothes to the ground.

Ashley gasped, as all ten men hopped upon the table. They attacked her like prisoners released from death row. Clipped at the knees, she was knocked to the surface.

Her dress was pulled over her head, left as a mask. She couldn't see a thing, though felt herself flipped over. As her hands were yanked behind her back, she was wrapped with telephone cord. Clearly, a few of the men had seen her bondage films.

Flipped back upright, another phone cord was tied in a figure-8 around her breasts. They swelled with pleasure. She felt two sets of lips engulf her stiff nipples, sucking and gnawing with teeth. Meanwhile, multiple sets of hands pulled her panties down to her stocking covered knees, tearing the G-string to shreds.

The dress was pulled further upward, exposing only her mouth. It still masked her nose and eyes. *These men are gonna make me earn this,* she thought to herself, causing her box to moisten.

She felt a large hand pry her lips and jaw open, simultaneously feeling her thighs pried as well. A massive cock was stuffed into her wet mouth. It sailed directly into her throat. Having no time to warm up, the professional cocksucker gagged like an amateur.

Before she knew it, another thick cock was thrust into her creamy cavern. Her body tensed, feeling the large spear bump her uterine wall. Both cocks pumped in countermeasures, disallowing her a break from constant use.

Having no idea of anyone's appearance, all she heard was a rush of eager voices. "My turn!"

"No, me next, asshole!"

"Move!"

The two intruders were suddenly withdrawn. She felt her body lifted up, laid on top of another man's body. His large cock poked her curved cheeks. Her legs were pried apart again, as two tongues invaded her jelly pastry. One licked her heavenly hole, while the other rimmed her savory star.

Both ended with pools of slick saliva injected into her. The next sensation was a cock eased into her anal cavity. Her sphincter was forced to accept the foreign idol, as it fought through the stubborn ring.

As one cock bottomed out, another slid into her vaginal valley. She was instantly filled in double penetration. Ashley cried out in lust, feeling every nerve and gland set aflame.

Right as her body accepted the pressure, another cock was shoved into her mouth. Every orifice was invaded. Her feet were wrapped around the top man's waist. Pressed together, she was commanded to give a foot job. The thin black stockings stroked a very long, thick cock. She had no way of visually measuring, though it was at least 9-inches in length.

The train rolled on, as a rotating schedule began. Each of the ten men took turns pumping every hole. Alternating sizes and depths forced Ashley's innards to keep adjusting, constantly stimulating her. Mrs. Taylor's tied breasts were sucked, pulled, slapped, bitten, and gnawed.

Just when she thought she'd faced every fire, along came another flame. Bodies began adjusting themselves, as a second cock was squeezed into her vagina. Then another was added to her mouth.

She was stretched beyond any limit she'd ever experienced. Her body suddenly burst into uncontrolled orgasm. An ocean of fluid squirted from her, though wasn't enough to expel the army inside.

For two hours, the sex parade marched on. She orgasmed vaginally, anally, and clitorally; cumming a record 20 times. After each one, she swore it was the last, until the next one was more intense.

Her senses were tortured with mixed signals. First it was hot, cold, warm and cool. Then hard, soft, scratched and slapped. Every emotion flowed through her veins. Right before she collapsed in exhaustion, all cocks were withdrawn. The blockade upon her eyes was removed.

Squinting from the sudden flash of blinding light, her vision adjusted to ten men kneeling around her. They were all nude, stroking their cocks over her. *Bukkake,* she silently thought, having never experienced it before. The same degradation, which made her avoid it, also caused her to drip with lust.

She focused on their multi-sized cocks, studying their various shades and shapes. Of course, only one color would exit them.

"Ah!" one man shouted, being the first to fire his load. It landed upon her vagina. A second man unleashed upon her face. The third covered her breasts. Next, her stocking feet were soaked. Rivers of white rain flowed upon her soft pale skin, covering every inch.

Shutting her eyes, Ashley was buttered in male lotion. Thomas watched in disbelief. At first he felt bad, though it all changed when he saw the glow upon her face. *She truly is a natural slut,* he told himself.

As the last loads slowed to a trickle, she shouted, "Untie me. Let me...touch it. Let me taste it!"

One of the stockholders reached underneath, untying her corded wrists. Her hands franticly massaged her slick body, roving every inch of liquid porcelain. Gliding down her stomach, she reached her vagina, slipping a finger inside. Having already cum so much, the last would be the greatest.

Stinging warmth tingled through her, as she convulsed in violent pleasure. Feeling her manicured fingernails slush the mixed cocktail inside sent volts of electric shock from head to toe.

Removing the finger, she scooped up more from her skin. Placing it in her mouth, her eyes rolled in delight. The men watched in animalistic lust, as she dined upon their offering. Any man, who once had doubts about their decision, was no longer on the fence.

Ashley Taylor was the future of porn, and the future of their company.

*****

The one-year mark arrived, as Ashley Taylor was finally free of Ethan's prison. She pulled up to her house, thankful to see it still intact. Contrasting the thoughts she had before servitude, *I'm glad to be home.*

As she entered the door, her children raced to her. They hugged her tighter than ever before. "Mom! We missed you!" her daughter said.

"Is your work trip done now?" her son asked.

"It is. How are you guys? Let me get a look at you...you're both so grown up!" she said, checking their eyes for any dilation or sign of highness. They appeared unaffected.

"We're not stoned," her son interjected. "Dad said we couldn't have any."

"Really? He was responsible?"

"He said we had to *buy* it from him. He wasn't sharing," the daughter said. "We don't get enough allowance."

"Then again, maybe not," Ashley said, still thankful for their sobriety.

Todd Taylor suddenly exited the bedroom singing, "Isn't it good...*Norwegian Wood*..." he paused in astonishment. He shouted,

"Holy piss! It's...a dream come true. A real life porn star in my living room! Thank the gods," Todd Taylor said, running to her.

"Porn star?" the son asked.

"He's having an episode again, kids. Go get ready, we're going out to eat."

The kids ran to their rooms, excited to eat an actual meal again.

"Are you here to bang me?" Todd asked. "Perform a *Dirty Sanchez*? I tried to bid in the auction, but I'd emptied my bank account on dope."

"Speaking of dopes...you're married!" she yelled, bopping him in the head. "I'm your wife!"

"Oh shit! I remember you now. I knew you looked familiar."

Having pondered the question for a while, Ashley finally decided to ask. "If you don't even remember we're married...then why the hell are we?"

He paused, searching his empty head. "Oh yeah, that also reminds me...I have some bad news."

"What?" she asked.

Todd fished papers from the drawer. "Juan!" he shouted.

"Who the hell is Juan? Are those divorce papers?"

A feminine man exited the bedroom. He wore leopard skin panties while blowing a cloud of toxic smoke. "Who's this bitch?" he said with flaming affect.

Todd cut in. "I'm leaving you for my dealer."

"You're gay?"

"No. I'm stoned...and he gives really good narcotic!"

"*Ho!*" Juan said, hissing at Ashley, forming a cat claw with his hand.

A stunned Mrs. Taylor signed the papers quickly. Afterward she said, "Kids. It's time to go now!"

The kids came out, as she led them to the door. "Where are we going?" they asked.

"To get antibiotics."

Todd called out. "Oh before you leave...did anyone ever tell you...you look just like that *one* porn star? I never did learn her name."

She stopped, turning back towards them with a smirk. "Yes...because I *am* her," she said, exiting.

Todd's mouth hung open, releasing a cloud.

"See, I told you she was a ho!" Juan said, snapping in a Z-formation.

*****

Eight Months Later

Ashley pulled her car into the company's parking lot. She parked in the best spot, reserved only for the boss.

Entering the office, Thomas Cole awaited her. The two paused, feeling a sudden spark hit them. A long absence didn't erode the feelings from their night together. They smiled at each other. "It's good to see you again," Thomas said.

"Follow me," she said warmly, leading him to her office. Upon entrance, Ashley sat in the seat behind the desk.

"How've you been? I haven't seen you in months...in person, at least. Though, your image has been everywhere."

"Been so busy with promotion, filming, family...I can barely get a moment to breathe anymore. I knew running a million dollar enterprise would take work...but damn."

"Well, I'd say it's paid off. I think you're owed a congratulations," Thomas said. "Did you see the stock price today? Through the roof! You did it!" he told her. "With the release of the latest earnings...*this* company has turned profit. Record time! You've made a believer out of Wall Street. You're rich!"

"Actually, that's why I invited you here," she said.

"To tell me you're rich? That's kind of conceited, don't you think?"

"No...to tell you that *you're* rich. It unfolded just like we planned. Your brother panicked at the initial dive. He practically begged me to buy, saying it would be the deal of my life."

"For once...he spoke truth."

"He didn't think I could do *his* job...believing I'd flop. He sold at the low, accepting a salary reduction until finding a new job. Right after that...word got out that this girl plays ball. No one would hire him."

A huge smile came to his face, "So you're saying he's your bitch?"

"Something like that," she said.

"So I can buy my shares back now?"

"No."

"I thought you said I was rich?"

"Thomas...I'm giving the company back to its original owner. You're getting the majority share."

"What?"

"I've made more money in one month than I'll ever spend...more than I'll ever need. Honestly, it's also more bullshit than I ever wanted."

"But...you're the face of this company...the talent!"

"Which I'll continue to be...on my own terms. Ashley Taylor will still do appearances and promo work, though my film days are over," she said. "I have kids to raise. Besides, this is your dream, not mine."

"Your husband can't help with the kids?"

"You mean ex-husband."

All the blood drained from Thomas's face. He'd only imagined such a thing in his dreams.

Mrs. Taylor handed over a paper to sign. "This will return the shares to the investors. I'll hang onto a few...for a rainy day. The rest belong to you, Mr. Cole."

His trembling hand went to sign on the dotted line. *This is your moment...just like Ashley in the conference room. Take the risk damn it!* The pen suddenly steadied, as he looked into her eyes. "What if it's not my dream anymore?"

"Isn't that why we did all this? So you could get it back?" she asked.

"In the beginning."

"Now?"

"Now...my dream is *you!*" he said with conviction. "The only way I'll take the company...is with you by my side. As my co-owner. As my wife."

She gasped. "I...I'm speechless," she said, as he approached her. "I don't know what to say?"

He lifted her from the chair, sitting down. Placing her on his lap, he placed a hand on her head. "Just like some nights can't be valued with money, some moments can't be described by words." He held her face, pulling her lips to him. The kiss was slow, sensual, and sexual.

As the kiss broke, they both shook with weakness. "Will you still want me when I tank the company like my brother?" Thomas asked.

"We'll just buy a marijuana farm. I know a guy...who'll keep us in business," she winked.

"Should we invite my brother to the wedding?"

"Speaking of the devil," she reminded herself, pressing the intercom button. "Mr. Cole, I'd like to see you in my office."

Within moments, Ethan Cole entered. "What do you need, Ashley?" he asked, lifting his head in horror. He dropped his papers to the floor, seeing his sibling.

"Hello brother," Thomas said. "It's been a while."

"That's Mrs. Taylor to you," Ashley corrected Ethan. "Get me a cup of coffee."

Ethan grimaced, following her order. Ashley stood up, pacing the room. She quietly went to the water cooler, reaching for a cylinder-shaped paper cup. Thomas squinted his eyes in wonderment.

"Here's your coffee," Mr. Cole said.

"Set it down."

He placed the mug on the oak surface. "Anything else you *require* of me?"

"Bend over the desk...and drop 'em."

"You mean...my pants?"

"Do you want this job or not?"

"You know I need the money!"

"Then listen to your boss."

Thomas looked over at her, she nodded in assurance.

Ethan shook in frustration, slowly exposing his ass. "I bet this gives you satisfaction!"

"I learned from the best," she said.

"Shit," he announced, leaning over.

A wicked smile crossed Ashley's lips, as she approached the hairy butt cheeks. Poking a hole in the cylinder cup, she self-lubed him with saliva. Spreading him wide, Mrs. Taylor eased it inside. Reaching for the coffee cup, she paused. "Thomas, can you do me a favor?"

"Anything."

"For this job...I think I'll need the entire pot."

"*No!*" Ethan Cole screamed in bloody murder.

Other Books by J.D. Grayson

More titles available on Amazon

YOUR FRIENDLY NEIGHBORHOOD BDSM CLUB
Available at: Amazon

After entering the local PTA meeting, Caroline Chase feels out of place. She finds an unwelcoming bunch of ladies, prim and proper in every manner. Owen Hayes, the dapper PTA president, presents the same air of perfection. Too good to be true, she knows the most polished people often hide the dirtiest secrets.

Intrigued by the group's plastic facade, Caroline Chase returns again. It's then, she finds a reality which only existed in her sexual fantasies. Challenged to submit, she'll be forced to face questions of inner strength and willpower. However, Caroline will soon discover, she's not the only one in need of an awakening.

*****

THE PREGNANCY TRANCE
Available at: Amazon

Amber Evans enters a hypnotherapist's office seeking help. Unable to get pregnant, she's desperate to find an answer. Eager to cure her, Bruce Carson examines her subconscious mind, treading a darker path than he expected to walk.

Fighting his own battle of darkness, Bruce hopes redemption lies in Amber's cure. Though to heal her, he'll have to survive the dangerous place it takes him. Obsessed with his mission, he'll even risk his life to deliver the pregnancy trance.

*****

MARRIAGE THERAPY: A DOM, A SUB & A CUCKOLD
Available at: Amazon

Lori and Tyler Hale have a nice home, good jobs, and decent relationship. Though while Tyler is happy to forego bedroom matters, Lori desires a kinky edge. With no answer in sight, the couple turns to marriage therapy.

Recommended by a friend, Dr. Stone welcomes the couple into his office. The Hales soon discover their therapist's unique way of treatment. Using the tools of sexual discipline, he pushes their marriage to the edge. Willing to risk their breaking, he challenges their sexual limits. Though the more he explores his female patient, the more he's tempted to let them fail.

*****

THE FANTASY FACTORY: EDGY ROLE PLAY
Available at: Amazon

Vicky Lane's sex life has hit a wall. Failing to spice things up with sexy outfits and toys, the luscious housewife threatens her husband with an affair. After he carelessly dares her to go forward,

Vicky calls Gavin's bluff. Raising the stakes, she lets her dark side shine.

She signs up for the fantasy factory, where fantasy becomes reality. Wanting to act out her darkest taboo, she signs her freedom away, putting it in the hands of unknown men. Taken at random, an edgy adventure follows suit. Vicky hopes to teach Gavin a lesson of her value, though by the end, the lesson will belong to them both.

The Fantasy Factory series will be an occasional series of non-sequential, "Paid for hire" role-play. They can be read in any order.

*****

DOCTOR MÉNAGE
Available at: Amazon

Returning to their hometown in style, Doctors Mason & Ross open a sexual medicine practice. Blessed with wealth and good looks, the bachelors are desired by every female in the zip code. Since the girls can't win the doctors' hearts, they must settle for sexual treatment instead.

Attending their high-school reunion, the doctors are approached by a face from their past. The popular and beautiful Kayla Carter seeks them out, hoping they'll cure her sexual dysfunction. Agreeing to treat her, the two doctors make a deal to stimulate her body, but not their hearts. Of course, promises are easier to make than keep.

*****

The Colony:
Arrival (Part I)
Temptation (Part II)
Prophecy (Part III)
Addicts (Part IV)
Available at: Amazon, Smashwords, iBooks & B&N

After years of marital heartache, Dylan & Alexa Hunter have lost the will to go on. After being approached by a mysterious man, they are offered a chance to start over in a utopian paradise. The word eternity is spoken, though left undefined.

On the island of Aionios, no fruit is forbidden, no pleasure denied. Accepting the tempting offer, the couple surrenders everything, including freewill itself. Though they'll soon learn that even paradise has a dark side.

*****

Slaves & Breeders:
Abducted into Sex Slavery (Part I)
Chosen to Breed (Part II)
Into the Fire (Part III)
Available at: Smashwords, iBooks & B&N

Having grown up in foster care, Haley White only knows disappointment. Cloaked in a mask of false strength, the troubled

127

teen enters a world of harsh reality. As she attempts to better her life, few opportunities open their door to her.

As the years tick by, the 21-year old discovers an ad for a modeling agency. Tired of working small jobs for small money, she agrees to a photo shoot. After being chosen for the position, her fate takes a frightening turn. Haley White is abducted.

Taken to a remote island, she's an immediate candidate to breed her new master's heir. However, her rebellious attitude will have to be broken first. Feeling helpless in her captivity, she finds that her captor shares a common bond.

*****

THE PATIENT:
PHYSICAL (PART I)
DOUBLE DOSE (PART II)
THE CURE (PART III)
Available at: Amazon, B&N, iBooks, Smashwords, KOBO, Sony, and Diesel

Twenty-two year old, Rebecca Stone is a naive girl with medical anxiety. Having minimal sexual experience, and being submissive in nature, she is prime meat in the hands of horny predators. Sensing her obvious weakness, her new boss demands a pre-employment physical. However, what she doesn't know, is that the doctor's secretly working with him, exploiting timid girls like herself.

Rebecca is forced to face her deep fear of doctors, pulled into a world of medical submission. Along the journey, she will discover the root of her feelings, and gain a newfound fetish in the process.

*****

TEACHING EMMA:
A CONTRACT OF SUBMISSION (PART I)
THE MASTER/SUB EXPERIENCE (PART II)
FREEDOM OF SUBMISSION (PART III)
Available at: Amazon, Smashwords, iBooks & B&N

Emma Heart starts college with an unusual elective: Human Sexuality-Fetish and Lifestyles. She doesn't know that her new teacher, Mark Ryan, is as unusual as the course itself. The class is given a contract of submission, agreeing to become his subs, empowering him their Dom. The lessons that follow will not be learned from books, but bodies.

As he focuses on Emma, Professor Ryan begins to question his own methods. Feeling stronger for his student than expected, he realizes the only outcome is heartbreak. He must decide between love or scholastic duty. The question is...can he?

*****

DOMINATED BY THE BOSS (PART I)
DOMINATED BY THE BOSS (PART II)
Available at: Amazon, B&N, iBooks, Smashwords, KOBO, Sony, and Diesel

After her husband loses his job, Ashley Taylor begins stealing from her company. What starts as petty theft, becomes grand larceny. Caught by her boss, Mrs. Taylor is faced with a simple choice.

Go to federal prison for many years or serve Ethan Cole for one? What appears to be the safe choice becomes a world of domination. Punished for her misdeeds, she'll discover that every dollar must be repaid. However, the currency is not money. It's her sexual freedom.

*****

THE HYPNOTIST: SEX TRANCE
Available at: Amazon

Hoping to cure his wife's bedroom boredom, Sean Day turns to hypnotherapist, Joseph Ryan, to cure his wife. Though, due to Misty's uptight upbringing, the hypnotist is forced to skirt the rules. He lies to her.

Under the guise of smoking addiction treatment, Misty is seduced into trance. Joseph intends to fix her intimacy issues. However, after exploring Misty's dark mind, a deeper issue is revealed. Her words unlock Mr. Ryan's own unspoken fetish, forcing him to break new ground. Pushed to the edge of submission, Mrs. Day will face her shameful secrets, along with the mental bonds that hold her captive.

About J.D. Grayson

Website: www.JDGraysonBooks.com
Twitter: @JDGraysonBooks
Facebook: http://www.facebook.com/JDGraysonBooks

You can contact J.D. Grayson at JDGrayson@hotmail.com

J.D. Grayson lives in the state of Florida, where the heat and sweat naturally lead him to write erotica. Preferring short erotica to long form, he tries to offer a burst of pleasure, while merging an interesting story with a few twists along the journey.

With every work, Grayson attempts to straddle the line of sensuality and kink, story and sex, as well as fantasy and reality. Although sex always leads the way, he strives to add imagination to every plot line, in addition to each sex act. Some stories are lighter in tone; others are darker, though he always aims for a tasteful presentation.

His ultimate goal is to add spice to the life of readers. In his daily conversations with "average couples," he discovered that the current state of sexuality is not in a good place. Somehow, it's been lost in maddening schedules, busy lives, and shamed stereotypes. Its importance and priority are pushed to the back burner, as a chore not a reliever.

If just one of his stories adds some lust to their love, then his mission is accomplished.

Made in the USA
San Bernardino, CA
01 September 2015